Death Comes Full Cycle

Remo saw the cyclists wheel for a return run. With a simple backhand snap, he took the first rider off his cycle and held him. Chiun was a bit more efficient. He let his cyclist continue with a minor alteration in the plastic shield over his face mask. There was a small hole in it the width of a forefinger. There was also a small hole in the forehead behind the mask. It oozed red as the driver, not caring anymore, zoomed complacently into a fire hydrant, where he became separated from his machine and sailed off into a pile of rotting garbage, with which he blended very well.

Remo's rider kicked and screamed. Remo held him by the neck. Sweetman tried to reach the rod in his jacket pocket. Unfortunately, Sweetman was now unqualified for holding a gun. His right arm ended in a bloody wrist . . .

The Destroyer

HOLY TERROR #19

by Richard Sapir & Warren Murphy

PINNACLE BOOKS • NEW YORK CITY

This is a work of fiction. All the characters and events
portrayed in this book are fictional, and any resemblance
to real people or incidents is purely coincidental.

THE DESTROYER: HOLY TERROR

Copyright © 1975 by Richard Sapir and Warren Murphy

An original Pinnacle Books edition, published for the
first time anywhere.

ISBN: 0-523-00640-3

First printing, June 1975

Printed in the United States of America

PINNACLE BOOKS, INC.
275 Madison Avenue
New York, N.Y. 10016

For Norm and Dolores, Andy and Ellen, Warren and Doreen, Lois, Joanne, Jim and Geri, and Meme, who was once called Mimi by mistake, and of course for the awesome magnificence of the glorious house of Sinanju, which sometimes recognizes the following post office box:

P. O. Box 1149
Pittsfield, Mass.
01201

CHAPTER ONE

Many things are holy, but few of them holy men.
— HOUSE OF SINANJU.

When the Reverend Titus Powell saw the bodies being loaded on ox carts in the outskirts of Calcutta, he asked himself if he were willing to die.

More specifically, was he willing to give up his life for a white girl?

Even more specifically, was he willing to give up his life for a rich white girl whose father, just two decades ago, had made Reverend Powell ask himself the identical question over the value of a cup of coffee. He remembered it clearly. You don't forget facing death.

"Ain't no one stopping y'all from drinking that cup of coffee, Reverend. But they ain't gonna be no one stopping them from hanging y'all from the big elm at Withers Creek neither."

Those had been the words of Elton Snowy, owner of Snowy's Pharmacy, Snowy's Mill, Snowy's Drive-in, and Snowy's Farm, in Jason, Georgia. Mr. Snowy, who was a Jason on his mother's side, had stood with the Silex still

1

bubbling at the lunch counter in his pharmacy, with the young Reverend Mr. Powell sitting in front of an empty coffee cup and a crowd of jeering white youths behind him.

"I'll take cream and sugar," Reverend Powell had said, and he saw the two dark barrels of a shotgun stuck in his face. On the triggers down the barrels was one fat pink finger. The nail was grimy. The nail, the finger, the hand, and the gun belonged to the saw mill foreman who, everyone in Jason knew, was the leader of the local Ku Klux Klan.

"One barrel or two with your coffee, nigger?" asked the foreman.

Reverend Powell heard the laughter behind him, saw Snowy hold the pot over the cup, smelled the aroma of fresh-ground coffee, and knew if he lived he would never drink coffee again.

"I said one barrel or two, nigger?" repeated the saw mill foreman.

"Get that outa here," yelled Snowy. "There'll be no shooting in this pharmacy."

"You gonna serve a nigger?"

"You ain't messing up this place with that double barrel."

"And you ain't gonna serve no nigger."

"Hey, Mr. Snowy," came an out-of-breath voice from the door of the drugstore. "It's a girl."

"If you think I'm gonna allow bloodshed in here the day my wife gives me a daughter, you're out of your cotton-pickin' head there," said Snowy. "Put that double barrel away, and let's all go to my place for a little real refreshment. I'm closing the pharmacy."

"All" of course did not include Reverend Powell. But in the general joy, he did get his cup of coffee, with no barrels.

"Just for this occasion," said the saw mill foreman,

2

pointing the shotgun at the cup. "It ain't gonna be no regular thing."

But the South was changing all over, and it did become a regular thing for the blacks in Jason to eat at the same counters and to go to the same movie theaters and to drink from the same fountains, and twenty years later, if anyone asked whether a black, least of all the Reverend Mr. Powell of Mt. Hope Baptist Church, could get a cup of coffee at Snowy's, a resident of Jason would have looked at the questioner as if he should be committed to an insane asylum.

Now, as the ox cart creaked by him on a foreign road in India, Reverend Powell remembered that long-ago day in Jason. He could see bodies dangling limbs from the cart in a looseness no living person could duplicate. Bellies swelled forward but ribs protruded, cheeks sunk beneath vacant eyes staring out into eternity, never to blink again.

The road smelled of human excrement, and the morning had no coolness to it, just a smothering heat that would become unbearable when the sun rose to its full powers. Reverend Powell felt his seersucker suit sticking to him as it had even yesterday, but so filthy had been the hotel the night before that he had not dared change it. He leaned against the gray 1947 Packard with the new coat of paint, a car that would have been junked back in Jason, and looked at the driver, a brown-skinned man with Caucasian features. The driver had stopped for a large gray cow with a dangling, fleshy throat. Just minutes before he had refused to stop for a baby crying in the street, because it was what he called "an untouchable." Cows were sacred in India. Bugs were sacred in India. Everything was sacred in India, thought Reverend Powell—everything but human life.

Instead of waiting in the car's greasy back seat for the cow to pass, Reverend Powell had gotten out, and when he saw the ox cart of bodies go by, he knew he had to

3

make a decision: go on, to what he felt now would be his death, or go back to Jason.

He still had several hundred miles along roads like these to reach Patna at the foot of the Vindhya Mountain Range, Patna on the Ganges up from Calcutta. Famine was upon the land despite gifts of American grain that rotted in warehouses of Calcutta and Bombay and Sholapur, despite even more grain that reached the people. Despite the most aid America ever gave any country it had not been at war with, India was still collecting its starved dead in ox carts while its sanctimonious ministers in New Delhi, who presumed to preach morality to the world, lavished money on atomic bombs.

Reverend Powell said a little prayer and steadied himself. The cow had to move soon, and he must decide whether to go on up the road to Patna or go back to the airport and return to where he could breathe the fresh air of the piny woods or share a mess of catfish with his family or cry out his love of God before his congregation in the neat white church set off on the grassy slope by the old Snowy Mill.

He felt that his life hinged on the decision he made, but just last week, it had not seemed all that terminal. Difficult, yes; terminal, no. He had regarded it all as an exercise in turning the other cheek.

"Reverend," Elton Snowy had said back in Jason exactly seven days before, "you gotta help me. I think maybe you're the only one who can. I got a letter here from Joleen. I think she's been, well, sort of kidnapped. Sort of."

"Joleen. Little Joleen. Why, she's such a lovely girl. A real Christian, if I may say so, Mr. Snowy."

"Yes sirree, a lovely girl, a lovely girl," said Snowy. Reverend Powell could see red rings around Snowy's eyes, as if the richest man in Jason had been crying.

"I need your help, Reverend. I know Joleen used to

4

sneak down to your section of town and do social work and all. And I know you and your people liked her."

"She is a lovely girl, Mr. Snowy. Can I offer you a cup of coffee? Myself, I haven't drunk any for twenty years."

"No, thank you kindly," said Snowy and pushed a worn letter at Reverend Powell. "Read this please. It's from Joleen to her ma."

Reverend Powell read the letter, and he was confused. It seemed like a pleasant enough message from a girl who had found happiness and communion with a divine force. What confused Powell was the reference to her father's good civil rights work, but that it was nothing compared to the work of the Blissful Master she had found there in Patna, India.

"If only your very close friend, Reverend Powell, could see the complete happiness of the Divine Bliss Mission here in Patna," the letter read, "I would be eternally grateful. For the sake of Jason, he should see it right away."

The printing on the letter said, "The Divine Bliss Mission," and according to its letterhead, it had offices in Paris, Los Angeles, New York, and London. Its home was Patna, India. A picture of a fat-faced teenage boy was engraved at the top of the letter. A fuchsia halo surrounded his head.

"I see your daughter has done what the Lord hath failed to wrought," said Mr. Powell pleasantly. "She has made me your close friend."

"It's a code, Reverend. She's in trouble. I'm not sure what kind of trouble, but she's in trouble. She thinks you're the only man who can save her. I don't know why. Maybe it's because those Indias are colored folk too. She's a good girl, Reverend. I know she's not your flock, but . . . but . . ." Elton Snowy turned away. "Please don't visit the sins of the father on the daughter."

5

"Why don't you go to one of these Divine Bliss Missions and ask about her yourself?"

"I did. I hired people. I hired lots of people. Two went to India. They never came back. They joined that little . . . that little Blissful Master."

"I see," said Reverend Powell. "Well, I remember the day Joleen was born. I was having a cup of coffee at the time."

"I'm not asking for myself. And if anything should happen, your family will be well provided for. You have my word on that."

"A passable nice offer, Mr. Snowy. But I know my family will be taken care of. Because if I go to find Joleen, you're going to deposit $50,000 in my lawyer's escrow account."

"I'll give it to you now, Reverend. Cash. I can get you that in cash."

"I don't want your money. I want security for my family if I should not be here to provide for them."

"Perhaps insurance. I could arrange a hundred thousand dollar policy, Reverend, and . . ."

"My lawyer's escrow account. If I should die, my family will be provided for. I'd rather not have to repeat myself, if you please, Mr. Snowy."

"Certainly. Certainly. You're a real Christian."

So now he was looking for Mr. Snowy's Joleen, and if it were a good deed, then certainly he should be able to trust in the Lord. If he had faith, both he and Mr. Snowy's daughter would be back in Jason by month's end. He would return Mr. Snowy's money, and perhaps it would give that acquisitive man a chance for the glory of charity. The church sure could use a fine new air conditioning system.

If he had faith. But it was so hard to have faith in the face of death.

The cow looked around condescendingly, then plodded

6

off along the dusty road, following the cart, which, if the cow had been hamburger the day before, would not now be full on its way to the body dumps.

"To Patna. On to Patna," said Reverend Titus Powell of Jason's Mt. Hope Baptist Church.

"I thought you might go back, you know," said the driver in a clipped British accent. "Most do when they see the carts."

"I thought about it."

"I hope you won't think less of India because of it. Really, almost all of them are untouchables and make no real contribution to the true grandeur that is India, don't you think?"

"I see men who died for want of food."

"Patna is a strange place for an African American," said the driver. "Are you going to see a holy man?"

"Perhaps."

"Patna is the home of holy men, ha-ha-ha," said the driver. "They know the government won't touch them there because of the prophecy. They're as important as the sacred cow there."

"What prophecy?" asked Reverend Mr. Powell.

"Oh, it's an old one. We have more prophecies than there is mud in the Ganges. This one, however, is believed by more than would care to admit, ha-ha-ha."

"You were talking about the prophecy."

"Ah, yes. Of course. Indeed. If a holy man, a true holy man, is harmed in Patna, then there will be the rumbling of the ground, and thunder from the east. Even the British believed it. In their reign there was an earthquake in Patna, and they looked high and low for a holy man. But all the wealthy, powerful holy men were well and in fine spirits. Then they found that the lowliest fakir, who lived at the foot of the mountains, had been robbed of one meal. His last meal. And soon after, the Japanese invaded. Then, again, a holy man had been doused in sweet oils

7

and set aflame because the concubine of a maharajah had said he had a beautiful spirit. And the Mongols invaded after that. Ever since, every enterprising holy order has had at least one home in Patna. The government respects them, yes, indeed."

"Do you know anything about the Divine Bliss Mission, Incorporated?"

"Oh, one of those American ones. Yes, very successful."

"Have you heard of the Blissful Master?"

"Blissful Master?"

Reverend Powell pulled Joleen's letter from his jacket. "His Indian name is Maharaji Gupta Mahesh Dor."

"The Dor lad, of course. Of course. If you can read and write English well, there is always work with him. And if you can . . ." The driver did not finish, and no matter how Powell pressed him, he would not answer what other sort of person could always find employment with the Dor lad.

Patna, like the rest of the famine areas of India, cleared away its dead in carts. An impatient Rolls-Royce dashed by them, and Powell's driver commented that it was a government minister on his way to Calcutta for an important conference on imperialist American atrocities, such as its failure to refinance a liberation library in Berkeley, California.

"It will be a good speech," said the driver. "I read where he is going to label the library closing for what it is—a genocidal racist repressive atrocity." The 1947 Packard took a little bump, and Reverend Powell's heart sank. The driver had not missed the little brown-skinned baby. Perhaps the child was better off.

"Well, here you are," said the driver, pulling up to a heavy wooden gate reinforced with large steel bolts, rising almost two stories into the air and flanked by white cement walls. It looked like a prison.

8

"Is this the Divine Bliss Mission? It looks like a fortress."

"To the Western mind, that which it does not understand is foreboding," said the driver. "It sees its own evil behind every obscurity. We do not have men with spears like your Pope."

Reverend Powell tried to explain that he was a Baptist, and therefore the Pope was not his spiritual leader, and anyway the Swiss Guards in the Vatican were only ornamental attractions with no intention of using any weapon. The driver seemed to understand all this until he was tipped, and, then, with a cheerio and a tally ho, he was off with a cry that the Papacy was a tool of the Central Intelligence Agency and all that rot.

Reverend Powell cried out after him that he wanted the driver to wait for the return trip, but he thought he heard only laughter from the coughing, sputtering 1947 Packard.

When Powell turned back to the door of the mission, he saw it had been opened. A pink-robed Indian priest, standing in the doorway, smiled. He had a silver streak painted down his forehead.

"Welcome, Reverend Powell. We have been expecting you, lo these many days."

Reverend Powell entered. He could not see people closing the high heavy wood and metal door, yet it moved slowly shut with a moan of its mass.

A splendid pink palace rose from the center of the courtyard, the Vindhya range looming snow-capped behind it in the distance. Shimmering reflections of colored glass played upon the pink, and at the center point of the palace, a crowning dome of golden brilliance forced the reverend to turn away his eyes.

"Uncle Titus, Uncle Titus. You're here. Wowee." It was a young woman's voice. It sounded like Joleen, but it came from a running maiden with very dark eyes and the cloppy run of sandaled feet. Her face was wrapped in pink linen, and a silver streak bisected her forehead. As she drew near, she said, "I guess I shouldn't say wowee anymore."

"Joleen. Is that you?"

"You didn't recognize me, I've changed so much, right?"

"Your eyes."

"Oh, the bliss perception." She took the strong, tired hands of Reverend Powell, maneuvered the worn wicker suitcase out of his grip, and with a short clap got the robed priest to run to them and pick up the valise.

"It looks like some sort of charcoal makeup over the eyelids," said Reverend Powell. He felt her nails play on his palm and instinctively withdrew his hand. She laughed.

"The eye makeup is only the external. You see the makeup with your eyes. But you do not see what goes on beneath my eyes, the eyes that swim under lakes of pure tingle."

"Tingle?" asked Powell. Was she trying to communicate in code? Was the eye makeup a narcotic? Was she bugged? This was all strange to Reverend Powell.

"The feeling behind my eyes. We were created to enjoy our bodies, not suffer with them. The Blissful Master, all praise be his name, has taught us to free ourselves. Tingle is part of the freedom."

"Yes, we got your letter—your father, my good friend, and I."

"Oh, that. All praise be the name of the Blissful Master. Praise be his infinite name and infinite being. He is wondrous in his life, and his life is our proof. Praise the blissful masterful life."

"Joleen, child, is there some place where we can talk in privacy?"

"Nothing is private from him who knows everything."

"I see. Then perhaps you would care to return with me tonight or as soon as possible, to spread the good word to

10

Jason," said Reverend Powell, scanning the walls. Standing along them were robed, turbaned men with unholy machine guns and bandoliers. The courtyard floor was delicate inlaid gold and red tile. Reverend Powell could hear the clod of his rough leather shoes as he walked with the girl who had been Joleen Snowy into the building under the golden dome. Inside, the Oriental splendor disappeared with a gust of cold air. He was walking on linoleum, with hidden air conditioning chilling him, and indirect lighting proving restful, if strange, to his eyes. It was good to be cold and dry, away from the hot, dusty death of the roads of India, away from the brown mud of the Ganges and the reek of human waste in body and in discharge.

Clear water bubbled from a clean chrome fountain. Set against a clear white formica wall was a red man-high soda machine.

"The Blissful Master believes that is holy which is made holy," said Joleen. "He believes we are here to be happy and when we are not, it is because we have poisoned ourselves in our minds. Don't be shocked by the modern heart of this palace. It is another proof of the Blissful Master's truth. Do you want a soda?"

"With all my heart, child, I would dearly love a soda. Do you have orange soda here in Patna?"

"No. Just Tab. The Blissful Master prefers Tab. If you want orange, go to Calcutta or Paris. Here we have Tab."

"I see the Blissful Master has a problem with calories."

"It is not a problem. A diet drink is a solution." Reverend Powell saw a flush creep up her soft pale cheeks. For the first time, he saw a strand of her golden yellow hair peek out from under her pink hood.

"We can leave to spread his word tonight, if you wish, child."

"You think I've been kidnapped, don't you? Don't you?"

Reverend Powell glanced around the large expanse of

11

the cool, white-walled room, like a horizontal snow pop set in a hot pink and brown dish that was India. Modern luxury in a continent of rancid death. If it were modern, it could have electronic listening devices. Suddenly he noticed cleanliness in the air. He was no longer smelling human excrement.

"Of course, I don't think you've been kidnapped. As I was telling your father, my close friend, I just want to come and see our little Joleen."

"Rubbish. Daddy isn't your friend. The day I was born it almost cost you your life to get coffee at his pharmacy. Daddy's a reactionary racist. Always has been. Always will be."

"But the letter, Joleen?" asked Reverend Powell, his mouth open in astonishment.

"Brilliant, wasn't it? Another proof of the perfection of our Blissful Master. He said you would come. He said Daddy would go to you and you would come here for me. He said you would do this at the request of a man who would have watched you die for a cup of coffee twenty years ago. Doesn't this prove his brilliance? Oh, perfection, perfection, perfection is my Blissful Master," shrieked Joleen, and she jumped up and down, clapping her hands in ecstasy. "A perfection. A perfection. A perfection. Another perfection."

From doors he had not seen, from drapes he had not noticed until they rustled, from stairways that had blended into the walls until he saw sandals coming down them, came young men and women, almost all of them white, a few black. None looked Indian except one girl who was more likely Jewish or Italian, thought Powell.

"Let me tell you another proof of our Blissful Master's perfection," Joleen announced to the throng and told about Jason, Georgia, and the history of the races, black and white, how distance had always been between them, but

12

the Blissful Master had said his perfection transcended races.

"And to prove it," shrieked Joleen, "here is a black man who has come at the bidding of my father, a white man and a hated segregationist. Lo, perfection we behold."

"Lo, perfection we behold," chanted the group. "Lo, perfection we behold." And Joleen Snowy led the Reverend Mr. Powell through the group of young people to two white doors that slid apart, revealing an elevator.

When the door shut them off from the crowd, Powell said, "I don't think deceit is a form of perfection. You lied, Joleen."

"It's not a lie. If you are here, isn't that a stronger reality, a stronger truth than a piece of paper? Therefore, a greater truth overcomes a lesser one."

"You sent a letter with deception in it, child. This deception is still a deception, still a lie. You never used to lie, child. What have they done to you here? Do you want to go home?"

"I want to achieve perfect bliss through the Master of Bliss."

"Look at me, child," said the Reverend Titus Powell. "I have come a long way and I am tired. Your father is worried about you. Your mother is worried about you. I was worried about you. I came because I thought you had been kidnapped. I came because your letter read like a code calling me to come. Now, do you want to go home with me, back to Jason?" He saw her head tilt and her eyes fix on his chest as her mind put together the intricacies of her answer.

"I am home, Reverend. And besides, you don't understand. You think it was what you call your Christian virtue that brought you here. It wasn't. It was the perfection of the Blissful Master, and I feel so happy for you,

13

because now you will enter bliss with us. And you almost missed it because of your age."

The elevator doors opened to a room furnished in chrome and black leather, deep chairs and long sofas, round glass tables and lighting that looked to Reverend Powell as if it had come from the pages of that fancy magazine he had once bought by mistake. He and Mrs. Powell had read it, laughing at the prices. You could buy a house for the cost of some of those furnishings.

He heard a mechanical "pong" from a far corner of the room, which smelled like lemon-scented Airwick.

"We're here," said Joleen. "The inner sanctum of the Divine Bliss Mission. Hail perfection, full of grace."

"Pong," came the noise again. Reverend Powell peered into the large, low room. The noise came from a machine. Two pudgy light brown hands twitched nervously at the sides of the cabinet.

"Pong," went the machine again.

"Shit," said a voice from behind the cabinet.

"Reverend Powell is here, O Blissful Master," chanted Joleen in a squeaky sing-song.

"What?" came the voice from behind the cabinet.

"Pong," went the machine.

"Reverend Powell is here as you predicted, O Perfection, O Enlightment."

"Who?"

"The one whom you perceived would come. The Christian. The Baptist whom we will show as a convert to our true enlightenment."

"What? What are you talking about?"

"Remember the letter, O Perfect One?"

"Oh, yeah. The nigger. Bring him in."

Joleen squeezed Powell's hand and with a beaming grin nodded to him to come along with her.

"I don't like that word. The last time it was used on me, young lady, was by rowdies in your father's pharmacy."

14

"You don't understand. 'Nigger' in the mouth of the Blissful Master takes the sting and prejudice from the word. What is the word but two insignificant sounds anyway? Nig and er. Nothing."

"It is not for you to decide. Nor for your master."

When Reverend Powell saw the Blissful Master, he nodded curtly and said, "uh huh," as if in confirmation. He was beyond shocks in this building. The Blissful Master wore a pair of too-tight white shorts and nothing else on a pudgy light brown body.

He looked like a knockwurst with a tight white Band-Aid around the middle. A youthful mustache struggled over precisely outlined lips. A lock of greasy black hair hung over his face. He stood before a television-type screen, watching a bouncing white blip and manipulating levers on both sides.

"Pong," went the machine, and the blip batted crazily from one side of the machine to the other.

"Just one second," said the youth, whom Powell judged to be fifteen or sixteen. The lad's lips twitched nervously. His English had only a trace of an accent, sort of English, like the white kids who had come down south in the summer to work for civil rights so long ago.

"Pong. Pong. Pong," went the machine and the Blissful Master grinned.

"All right, you're the nigger. Let's get to work. I'm Maharaji Gupta Mahesh Dor. Blissful Master to you."

Reverend Powell sighed, a tired sigh, hundreds of miles of dusty Indian roads, he sighed. Nights sleeping in the back of a car, he sighed. Watching the human monuments to famine being carried away, he sighed. The worry about the white girl who had once been so kind and so friendly to everyone. All these things he sighed and felt very tired when he spoke.

"Turkey, work your hustle on some other street. My

15

soul belongs to Jesus. And you, Joleen, I'm sorry for you. This is no spiritual man."

"Good," said Maharaji Dor. "We can dispense with the bullshit. The deal is this. You and I could jaw for a hundred years on St. Paul versus the Vedantic scriptures or whatever shit goes down nowadays. My deal is this. I know the way you should live to make you happy. That's it. Your tongue is designed to taste. Your eyes to see. Your legs to move. And when they don't do all these things, then something is wrong, right?"

Reverend Powell shrugged.

"Right?" said Maharaji Dor.

"Eyes see and legs move when God wills it."

"Good enough. Now ask yourself about the whole package. Are you supposed to walk around with the feeling that you're unhappy? That something's wrong? Unfulfilled? Nothing is ever as good as you thought it would be, right? Right?"

"Jesus is as good as I thought he would be."

"Sure, because you never met him. If that Jewboy were around nowadays, he'd be here if I got hold of him. Not hanging with nails in his hands. I mean, baby, what kind of deal is that? I'd never give you that deal."

"Praised be the Blissful Master," said Joleen clapping.

"Quiet, child," said Reverend Powell sternly.

"What I'm laying down is that I make you feel like you ought to feel. Your body is going to tell you I'm right. Your senses will tell you I'm right. Just don't try to turn 'em off. But if you do, I'll win anyhow, because I am the way. Dig?"

"Blissful Master," cried Joleen and threw her pink linen head wrapping at the two pudgy brown feet. Her blond hair settled over the pinkness of her sari. Reverend Powell saw her young breasts quiver under the dress.

Maharaji Dor snapped his fingers, and Joleen ripped the sari from her body. She stood pale and nude, smiling

16

proudly. Like showing a tomato for sale, Maharaji Dor squeezed the left breast.

"Good stuff," he said.

Reverend Powell saw the pink crest of her breast harden between brown thumb and forefinger.

"You think she doesn't like this?" said the boy. "She loves it. So what's wrong? Right." Squeeze.

Reverend Powell turned away. He was not going to be put upon by arguing with these heathens.

"Want this stuff? Take it."

"Good night, sir, I'm leaving," said the Reverend Mr. Powell, and the Dor lad smiled. As Powell turned, he felt two hands at his elbows, and as he struggled, he felt a collar being placed around his neck and locked, and his hands were shoved into shackles and pulled down behind him. His head fell backward, and his feet were being tugged. He braced his body for the cracking fall, but he landed on softness. Even the hand shackles were soft as they tugged at his wrists. He tried to get his legs under himself, but they went out in soft bindings to the right and left. Hands worked at his clothes, unbuttoned the jacket and shirt, and in a way he could not fathom, they got his clothes off his wrists and ankles without removing the shackles. He saw the lights from the ceiling and the soundproofing mosaic set around the strips of light.

He saw Joleen's face right above him. He saw her tongue dart out and felt it in the center of his head. Her firm breasts brushed his chest, and her tongue moved down his nose to his lips. They parted his lips briefly. He turned his head away and felt the wet tongue on his neck.

"Some things you can turn, nigger, and some things you can't," said Maharaji Dor.

The tongue tickled the reverend's belly button, and by the time it reached his loins, he knew he was out of control.

"I see your body is telling you something, nigger. What

17

do you think it's telling you? You know what it's telling you? You think it's wrong. You think you know better than the body God gave you, you say. When you need air, you need air. When you need water, you need water. When you need food, you need food. Right?"

Reverend Powell felt the moist hot lips closing on him now. He did not want it to be nice. He did not want it to excite him, to grab him, to move him, to bring him to the trembling edge of exquisite tension. And then the mouth was gone, and he was still wanting. Quivering out there, his body begging.

"More, please," said Reverend Powell.

"Finish him," said Maharaji Dor.

As the exquisite, surging, pounding relief consumed him, Reverend Powell began to feel his own wrath upon himself. He had failed himself, his God, and the girl he had come to save.

"Hey, baby, don't sweat it," said Maharaji Dor. "Your body's healthier than you are. You feel bad, not because of your body, but because of your big, big pride. Pride, Christian. You put your head on the block for a cup of coffee, but it wasn't for civil rights. What sort of man looks down the barrel of a gun and says, "Shoot"? A man who feels inferior? Bullshit. You knew damned well you were the best sonofabitch in that drugstore. Big hero. Same reason, hero, you came here for the blond twiff, what's her name? You were being the great Christian. Turning the other cheek to the richest white man in that town, what's its name? Right? Big man.

"When the young loudmouths started calling you Uncle Tom, you didn't mind. You knew they didn't have the balls to do what you did. Look down the barrel of a shotgun and order coffee, big man. They had the beads and the clothes and the raised fists, but you had God. Wonderful Titus Powell. I'll tell you what you're doing here. You came here to prove you're just the most wonderful nigger

18

in God's kingdom. Well, you black bastard, you ain't getting your pride massaged with any shotgun here. You ain't gonna get martyrdom here. No lynch mob. You're getting what you've run away from all your life. So first, we get rid of the damned guilt."

A pricking sensation in his right arm and then a rushing surge of everything being all right filled Reverend Powell. His fingertips felt a tingle and his knuckles felt a tingle and his wrists were alive and calm as were his forearms. His shoulders that had known so much lifting in his life eased into beautiful floating joints, and his chest became like bubbles beneath the ice of a frozen, smooth lake. His legs melted into the floor, and he felt cool fingers apply ointment to his eyelids, and then there were stars, tingling beautiful stars. It was heaven he was in, and there was a voice. A hard, rasping voice, but if you said yes to that voice, everything was all right again. And the voice was saying he should do whatever the Blissful Master said he should do. The bliss continued for "yes" and ended with "no." Reverend Powell thought it might be minutes or it might be days. The faces above him changed, and once he thought he saw night through a very close window. In it all, he tried to tell God he was sorry for his pride and that he loved Him and that he was sorry for what his body was doing.

Every time this happened, Reverend Powell felt the bliss leave, and when he cried out Jesus' name, there was downright pain. His palms felt crushed with heavy needles, and he cried the name again. And his legs felt a snapping of bone and the crushing through of iron, and with the total breath of his lungs, Reverend Titus Powell cried out the love of his lifelong friend. "Jesus, be with me now."

And then there was a sharp piercing in his right side, and before the dark eternity of nothing, he thought he heard his very best friend welcome him home.

19

Maharaji Dor was at his electronic game, winning, when one of his priests told him of the failure.

"What do you mean, he's dead? He just got here."

"A week he's been here, Blissful Master," said the priest, bowing a shaved but sweating head.

"A week, huh? What did you do wrong?"

"We did as you prescribed, Blissful Master."

"Everything?"

"Everything."

"What do you know? Huh? Well? Huh? Does the government know about this? Any word from Delhi?"

"We have no word, but they will know. The passport office will know. The foreign office will know. The Third World representative will know."

"All right. That's 300 rupees right there. Anyone else?"

"The Third World representative will want more. While the Reverend Powell might have been a United States citizen, by virtue of his blackness he was also a member of the Third World."

"Tell the Third World representative that he's only getting the hundred rupees to keep quiet because what's his name had an American passport. Tell him if he had been African, there wouldn't even be a pack of cigarettes for him in this, dig?"

"As you command."

"How'd the twiff take it?"

"Sister Joleen?"

"Yeah, her, Jo whatever."

"She cried because she said she truly loved Reverend Powell and now he had lost his chance at bliss."

"Good. Get lost."

"I am still worried about the government."

"Don't be. There isn't anything 300 rupees won't buy in Delhi, and besides, we got the prophecy. They're worried about China. They're not going to hassle us. We're holy men, dig? And they can't pester a holy man in Patna.

20

You'll see. The bread is just to keep things smooth. They really believe that bullshit legend."

"PONG, PONG, PONG." The machine suddenly moved without a lever being pulled. The blip circled crazily, and the glass of the screen rattled, and overhead the indirect lighting cracked out of the wall. There was sudden darkness and then flying glass, and the priest and Maharaji Gupta Mahesh Dor were tumbled like apples down a ramp toward the far wall, where they lay for hours until hands lifted them up.

The Maharaji heard how lucky he had been. Not everyone had survived the earthquake in Patna, and the next day, government officials arrived to examine the bodies of the holy men who had been killed. All of them who had died, however, had died in the earthquake. No holy man's death had been the cause of it.

No government official, no policeman or soldier or representative of the prime minister herself, bothered to check the ox carts as they squeaked out of town to the dumping pits. So they did not see the one much-darker body at the bottom of the pile of untouchables, the one with pierced palms and legs and the wound in his side.

It had been such a terrible earthquake, they had thought at first that the holiest men had died. But apparently this was not so, especially since the border with China remained quiet. There would be no terror from the east.

But east, even east of China, in a small town on the coast of North Korea, a message arrived. The Master of Sinanju would be returning home soon, because his employment would be bringing him to India, some incident in Patna that was of concern to his employer. On the way there, he would be given, in tribute to his glorious service, a triumphant return to the village his labors had supported for so many years.

CHAPTER TWO

His name was Remo, and he was bored with lacquered plates flying at his head, the ones with the fanged jaws of a dog inlaid over a calla lily background, the ones that came zipping in, sometimes with a curve or a dip or a hop, and sometimes straight for the cranium with enough speed to crack a skull.

Remo's left hand seemed to float up and gently touch most of the plates. Some of the plates he did not bother to block, and in the plates that were not blocked was the skill he was reminding his muscles and nerves to perform. Skill was not muscle but timing, and timing was merely being in unity, making and then keeping his perceptions in tune with reality.

This act of keeping the death plates from harming him reminded him of a simple lesson long ago when the Master of Sinanju had used slow bamboo spears that had at the time looked so fast that Remo had stood in terror as they came at him.

But these plates came five times as fast, just slower than a .22 short bullet. They whacked into the pillows behind him, tearing plush red fabric and snapping the springs of the couch. But the lesson he had learned from the bamboo staves was still the lesson now. Do not defend where you are not, but only that which is valuable to you. The hooking, dipping plates would only harm him if he went at the plates themselves, instead of staying within the zone of his body, and merely protecting it from the plates' intrusion.

The last plate came horizontal at his eyes, seemed to hang for a moment, then arched above his right ear and rose cracking into the wall, which opened a three-foot seam in the white plaster wall of the Rhoda Motel in Roswell, New Mexico. Outside was the Rio Hondo, a slip of a rocky stream that only in this parched summer would be called anything more than a brook.

"Home run," said the hurler of the plates, whose joy, unmitigated and mounting, had made Remo's life hell. If one had to have hell, Remo had thought, why must it be in New Mexico? But that was where he had been told to be and that was where he was. Chiun, the hurler of plates, did not mind being in New Mexico. He was going home to his native village of Sinanju in Korea, which his labors supported, just as the services of his father and his father's father and ancestors back to the earliest recorded time had supported the village.

Chiun was but the latest Master of Sinanju, and the services of the Master of Sinanju were always needed by one emperor or another. By czar and emperor, pharaoh and king, president and ethnarch, there was always work for the assassin, and the ancient House of Sinanju, sun source of all the martial arts, was simply the world's oldest, established, permanent repository of the assassin's skill. For hire.

In America, the services that had been hired were slightly different from usual. The Master of Sinanju had been retained to train one man, a white man, a man who

24

had been made publicly dead, an electrocuted man. Remo —who was then Remo Williams.

And in the years that followed, the training changed the very nervous system itself so that the body and the mind of Remo could see plates come at him and know instantly which required his body's attention and which he could safely ignore.

"It's no home run, Little Father. The pitcher doesn't get home runs. The batter gets home runs."

"You change the rules on me because I am Korean and not expected to know. I am being cheated of home run," said Chiun, and he folded his long delicate fingers over each other so that his golden kimono with the white butterflies settled in repose. Even his wispy ancient beard seemed to rest triumphant. The Master of Sinanju had caught his pupil in an injustice that he was savoring.

It had been like that since Chiun had been informed that since Remo would be going to Patna, India, going west over the Pacific, they would be going near Japan and Korea, and Chiun would be allowed to visit his home village of Sinanju, even though it was in the politically unfriendly northern part of Korea.

Since that day that Upstairs had gotten riled over something that had happened in India—why India, Remo didn't know, since India had about as much to do with Upstairs' mission as potato soup did with the hypotenuse of a triangle—since that day Chiun had been collecting injustices, the long-suffering Korean in a land of white racists.

He would return to his village to tell them what he had endured for them, while hiring out his talents so that the payments could support the aged and the infirm and the poor of the village of Sinanju.

"If I were white, it would be a home run," said Chiun.

"First, Little Father, we were exercising. I was, at least. And we weren't playing baseball."

25

"You wouldn't play with a Korean. Like your Little League. I understand. You whites are all alike. Bigoted. Yet, I maintain myself above your pettiness."

Through the crack in the motel room wall, a face peered. As the face retreated, Remo and Chiun saw a ten-gallon Stetson on top of the face that was on top of a bare chest, bare waist, and bare everything else. The man retreated further from his side of the wall. There was something on the bed, however. Blond and ass sassy and nude as a defrocked tick.

"Hi, there, fellas," she cried.

"Shut your mouth, woman," said the man from under the hat. He turned back to the wall. "You there. You and the gook."

"Aha," said Chiun. "Gook."

"Shit," said Remo.

"You heard me. Gook. Gook. Gook."

"Aha. Aha. Aha," said Chiun. "I stand here humbly insulted. Yet enduring, for I am a man of peace. Of love. Of tranquility."

"Here we go," said Remo.

"You make this hole in the wall?" asked the man under the hat.

A long, bony finger disengaged from the tranquility of rest with the other hand and pointed accusingly at Remo.

"You did, fella, right?" said the hat to Remo.

"You have brought grief into my life," said Remo.

"You want gree-yuf? You gonna get gree-yuf," said the man under the hat, and Remo saw him put on tooled leather cowboy boots, pick up a shiny six-shot revolver from the clothes pile, and walk out of sight. Remo heard the door in the next room open and close and then heard a knock on his door.

"It's not locked," said Remo.

The man entered, six-feet-four of him, six-feet-eight of him in his boots. The gun pointed at Remo's head.

26

"You sumbitch, you fuck round with me and my woman, I blow yo' head off."

"You do it, Clete," shrieked the girl through the broken wall. "You down and do it. Shoot me somebody. If you love me, you'll shoot me somebody." She bobbled off the bed, her chest poppity popping up and down in front of her. She stuck her face close to the hole in the wall. Remo could smell the sickening booze on her breath.

"Which one you want first, Loretta?" said the man with the gun.

"The violence of Americans is shocking," said Chiun.

"Get the little talky gook, honey," said Loretta.

"Violence against a minority," intoned Chiun. "Whipped and scorned and abused."

"When have you ever been scorned, abused, or whipped? No Master of Sinanju has ever suffered," said Remo.

Clete cocked his gun. Chiun looked heavenward in beatific innocence. A martyr to violent racism. There was one small drawback to his suffering. As the gun cocked, ready and raised, and the finger closed on the trigger, a white plate moved at such a speed that its blur followed it and made its way underneath the hat to where Clete's mouth had been, to where Clete's cheek had been, so that now there was the hat and the top half of a face biting down on a white plate filling red with blood and the remnants of a lower jaw spread out red and bone fragments on a hairy chest. The gun dropped, unfired.

"Drat damn," said Loretta. "I never get anything I want. Clete? Clete? Clete?"

Clete went forward, clumping into the gray-carpeted floor. Around his head, the gray darkened in an ever widening pool.

"He couldn't raise it too good, neither," noted Loretta. "How 'bout you fellas, you want a piece?"

"A piece of what?" asked Chiun, who was suspicious

27

of all Western dietary practices. He had promised Remo a real meal when they got to Sinanju, glory home of the East, pearl of the West Korea bay.

"A piece of me, pops."

"I am no cannibal," said Chiun, and Remo knew that this offer would also be included in tales of America . . . how some not only were cannibals, but some were volunteer dinners. This strangeness did the Master of Sinanju commit to memory.

"Oh, no, not that," said Loretta and made a circle of her left forefinger and thumb and rapidly penetrated and withdrew her right forefinger. "This," she said.

"You have done nothing to deserve me," said Chiun.

"How 'bout you, cutie?" she said to Remo, who stood just about six feet tall, with a lean, sinuous body that aroused many women just when he walked in a room. His eyes were dark, deep-set above high cheekbones, and his thin lips creased in a small smile. His wrists were thick.

"I've got to get rid of the body," said Remo, looking at the nude, dead man.

"No, you don't. There's a reward for him. Clete's wanted in three states. You're gonna be famous. Famous."

"See what you did," said Remo, and Chiun turned his head away, above it all.

It was a good thing, thought Remo, that the room was only a meeting place and that none of Chiun's heavy baggage accompanied them.

"Where are you two running to? The television cameras will be here. The reporters too. You'll be famous."

"Yeah, great," said Remo, and they went quickly down the motel hallway with the blonde yelling after them. They moved in such a way that the blonde thought they took off up the road for Texas when they really slipped down into the parched bed of the Rio Hondo and moved upstream along the bleached gravel 200 yards west of the motel, and there they waited and saw policemen and am-

28

bulance and newsmen. And on the second day, when a particular gray Chevrolet Nova came up the road, Remo ran out of the river bed and flagged it down.

"A little incident, Smitty," said Remo to the lemony-faced man in his late fifties, heading off any questions about why he was not in the prearranged motel room.

Remo signaled Chiun to follow him to the car, but the Master of Sinanju did not move.

"Will you come on? We've already spent a night in a frigging ditch because of you."

"I would talk to Emperor Smith," said Chiun.

"All right," said Remo sighing. "He'll only talk to you, Smitty."

As Remo watched Smith's gray head disappear into the river bed behind a large brown bush where Chiun sat, he could not help but think of the first time he had seen Smith. Remo had just come to in Folcroft Sanitarium on Long Island Sound, so many years before. As it was explained, Remo had been recruited, via a phony electrocution for a framed-up murder, to work for a secret organization, one that would work quietly outside the law to help give the law a better chance to work.

Smith was the man who headed the organization, and, besides Remo and the president of the United States, was the only person who knew it existed. Remo had lived with the secret for years. He was officially dead, and now working for an organization that did not exist. He was its one-man killer arm, and Chiun his trainer.

Remo watched Smith trudge back up the wash.

"He wants an apology," said Smith, who wore a gray suit and white shirt even in Roswell, New Mexico.

"From me?"

"He wants you to take back your racist remarks. And I think you should know we value his skills highly. It was a great service he did making you what you are."

29

"What was I while all this was going on? An innocent bystander?"

"Just apologize, Remo."

"Go dip a donkey," said Remo.

"We're not getting out of here until you apologize. Frankly I'm surprised that you are a racist. I thought you and Chiun had become very close."

"You're off limits," said Remo. "This is our thing. You don't understand it, and you don't have any business in it." Remo picked up a pebble and at 20 yards split a cactus at its base.

"Well, unless you apologize, all of us are going nowhere," said Smith.

"Then we're going nowhere," said Remo.

"Unlike you two, I happen to need water and shelter and food at reasonable intervals. Besides, I don't have a week to wait in a New Mexican river bed."

"With all your computers back at Folcroft, you don't need to know what we're all doing out here?"

"From what I gathered from Chiun, you're here because you changed some baseball rules on him and got another white to side with you. I gather he might be willing to forget this if a proper apology were offered. Something to do with tokens."

"Feed this into your computer. The last time Chiun wanted a token, it turned out to be Barbra Streisand. You ready for that?"

Smith cleared his throat. "Go tell him you're sorry so we can get on with the matter at hand. There's work to do. Important work."

Remo shrugged. He found Chiun where the Master had been sitting, his legs folded under him, his arms at rest on his lap, the dry desert breeze playing with his wisp of beard. Remo spoke to him only briefly and returned to Smith.

"Get this. The token he wants to mend his hurt is

fourteen fatted cows, a prize bull, flocks of ducks, geese and chickens in the hundreds, bolts of silk the length of castle walls, or Folcroft's walls since he still thinks of the sanitarium cover as a castle, ten handmaidens and a hundred carts of our finest brown rice."

"What's that?" said Smith, unbelieving.

"He wants to bring it home to Sinanju with him. That was your mistake, telling him last week he could visit his village. Now he wants to bring home something to show that his time in the West hasn't been wasted."

"I already told him you've got to go in by submarine. That's how the gold is delivered to his village. I think it's enough. You know we're supposed to be a secret organization, not a circus. Tell him providing transportation to take him home is enough."

Remo shrugged again, and again returned to Chiun, and again returned with an answer.

"He says you're a racist too."

"Tell him we just can't make the delivery of all that stuff, not until we establish diplomatic relations with North Korea. Tell him we'll give him a ruby the size of a robin's egg."

Chiun's response through Remo was that every Master of Sinanju who had ever ventured across the seas before had returned to Sinanju with tributes to his glory. All except the one who was unfortunate enough to work for racists.

"Two rubies," said Smith.

And when it was agreed under the hot New Mexico sun that the tribute to Chiun would be two rubies, a diamond half their size, and a color television set, Smith was informed that the good thing about Americans was their ability to see the flaws in their character and to attempt to amend them.

In the car Smith outlined the problem. CURE, the organization he headed and for which Remo and Chiun worked, had lost four agents checking out the Divine Bliss Mission, Inc. While the criminal potential for the DBM, Inc., was minimal, just another money hustle, its implications worried Smith. Thousands of religious fanatics loosed upon a country and directed by—there was no other word for it—a hustler.

Chiun, in the back seat, thought this was horrible.

"There is nothing worse than a hustler," said Chiun. "Woe be to the land to which a hustler comes, for the fields will lie fallow and the young maidens will abandon their chores for the flimsiness of his words."

"We thought that you, with your knowledge of the East, would be especially valuable in this, beyond just your training of Remo," said Smith, checking his rear-view mirror. Remo had early observed how Smith drove; every ten seconds he looked in the rearview mirror and for every five looks in the rearview mirror, there was a glance in the outside mirror. He drove this way on a high-way or in a driveway, a routine, controlled discipline that never varied. The dead president who had started CURE had picked the right man for the job, a man of stern self-control, a man whose ambition would never drive him to use the organization to control a country, a man incapable of ambition because ambition implied imagination, and Remo was sure that the last fantasy that had ever entered Smith's crusty New England mind was goblins in the closet and would Mommy turn on the light so they would go away.

"Sinanju is here to serve in truth and honesty," said Chiun, and Remo looked out the window, nauseated.

"Which is why I told Remo we would provide you with a trip home as a bonus for the wonderful job you've done with him."

"It has not been easy, considering the condition of the material," said Chiun.

"We knew that, Master of Sinanju," said Smith.

"Speaking of hustlers," said Remo, "what size rubies are you getting, Chiun?"

"There is a difference between accepting tribute and hustling, but I would not expect a racist to understand that. Emperor Smith, who is not a racist, understands this. He understands the meaning of tribute so well that to enhance his position in the grateful village of Sinanju, he may make the tribute three rubies and a diamond, instead of two rubies and a diamond, which is what the Chinese would probably pay. Such is the decency, Remo, of the most honorable Harold W. Smith, director of Folcroft Sanitarium—a man more fit to rule than your president and a man who need but say the word and this injustice of rule could be amended."

Smith cleared his throat while Remo chuckled.

"Getting down to business," Smith said, "we've been lucky. Somehow one of the Divine Bliss converts has defected. He was in Patna and was sent back to help work out what the Blissful Master's followers call some kind of big thing. The man had been elevated to, I think they call it, arch-priest. We're not certain. As you know, our organization works without people knowing what they're doing."

"Right through the top, Smitty."

"I was about to say, except for you and me. Chiun, as you know, thinks I'm an emperor."

"Or a mark," said Remo.

"A fine emperor," said Chiun. "One whose generosity marks him for eternal fame."

"One of the people who provides us with information, without knowing it, works in the newspaper business on the coast and somebody told him of something big, very big about to happen in America, and that only someone as shrewd as the Blissful Master could pull it off. The biggest ever, he said."

"The biggest what?" asked Remo.

"That's what we don't know. We do know that with an army of religious fanatics, it could be almost anything. Which is why we set the meeting at the Rhoda Motel. This Divine Bliss thing, it has so many people around that I didn't trust any of the usual channels. So I set up the meeting for here. Frankly I was a little worried when I saw you in that ditch waiting for me. The Blissful Master had one of his followers, a sheriff, put out a warrant for the defector. Three states. Poor devil was in hiding. We arranged to hide him near you, so you could question him. I'm sure your questioning techniques can get anything."

"The defector? His name Clete?" asked Remo.

"That's his hiding name."

"His girlfriend's name Loretta?"

"Yes, yes. Correct."

"He a big guy? Six-feet-four in bare feet?"

"Yes. You've met him?"

"He wear a Stetson?"

"Yes. That's him."

"Did he have a dish in his mouth and through the spinal column in the back?"

"No. Of course not."

"He does now," said Remo.

Chiun looked upon the blue heavens of New Mexico and the plains beyond. In the racist white man's country, who knew what they would accuse a poor Korean of next?

CHAPTER THREE

"So that's what you were doing in the river bed," said Smith when he heard about the plate incident. "Maybe we should get off the road. They might have the motel staked out. You might be spotted."

"We might also be tailed," said Remo.

"Anything is possible in a racist country," said Chiun, "where nude people invade your privacy."

Behind the gray Chevrolet Nova, a cream and beige Ford with a red bubble light on top and heavy black lettering just above the grill that read "Sheriff" cruised behind them. When Remo turned to look, the sheriff's car whined its siren and picked up speed.

"That may be the sheriff who is working for the Blissful Master," said Smith.

"Good," said Remo.

"Good? My Lord, they've got me with you. You know evasive techniques. I don't. Great. That's all I need, to be arrested in New Mexico."

"You like to worry, don't you, Smitty?" said Remo. "Just give me the outlines of the assignment and stop worrying."

"Find out what that Indian faker is doing with Americans. Find out what this 'big thing' is, and stop it if it's dangerous."

"Why didn't you say that before?" said Remo, "Instead of committing us to a trip to Patna, and all this submarine and side excursion to Sinanju bilge?"

"Because our emperor in his wisdom," said Chiun, "has blessed us with his brilliance. If we are ordered to Sinanju, then to Sinanju we will go."

"There'll be a sub, the *Harlequin,* at the naval base in San Diego. The captain will think you're from the State Department on a secret mission. He'll assume it's a quiet overture to establish relations with a North Korean faction for eventual diplomatic recognition."

"I still don't understand why we're hitting Sinanju," said Remo. "Other than it being closer to India than to Kansas City, why do we have to make the visit?"

The sheriff's car pulled alongside and a craggy-faced man under a light brown Stetson motioned the car to pull over. He motioned convincingly with a .44, whose barrel looked like a tunnel.

"Don't be shy, Remo. Chiun already warned me that you were thinking of dropping out to visit Sinanju yourself, the home of your training. And you're just valuable enough that we didn't want to lose you. So when this thing came up in India, I thought we could kill two birds with one stone, so to speak."

Remo glanced balefully at the back seat, where Chiun, his parched, delicate face set serenely, was a vision of calm innocence. Smith slowed the car.

"Get me out of this thing," he said as the sheriff's car nosed in ahead of them.

"Anyone who'd believe that I would quit you to visit a fishing village in North Korea, a village that has such lousy fishermen it has to rent out assassins to stay alive,

36

anyone who'd believe that could use help crossing a street."

"I can't be arrested," said Smith.

"If this is our sheriff, he's a gift," said Remo.

"That," said Smith, squinting at the man with Stetson, badge, and gun, stepping from the car, "is our man. Probably, I think."

"All right, you there. Out of the car slow, and let's see your hands at all times. Out," said the sheriff.

"You want to see my hands?" said Remo, putting them in front of Smith on the steering wheel and then sliding past Smith with his legs following through the window and out, a one-hand grip on the door post, and the feet touched the ground.

"How'd you do that thing? Jeez, like you just went through the window!" The sheriff stepped back to keep the trio covered.

"You want to see my hands?" asked Remo.

"I want to see all hands."

Smith put his on the steering wheel, flat out, thumbs spread. Chiun's long-nailed, delicate fingers rose to the closed window next to him and, opening slowly like a blossom, came to repose within themselves, fingers locking fingers until it looked as if two hands formed one fist. The sheriff seemed entranced for what he thought must have been less than a second, for he had been trained never to take his eyes off men he had covered. It was less than a blink of an eye, he was sure. But it must have been more. The young white man had his gun wrist, and then the fingers couldn't move or squeeze, and he couldn't even get a good kick at the guy because he didn't see him. But he felt him behind at his neck, and at his spinal column he felt two sharp pains, and his legs were out of control, walking him to the car, where the old gook had the door opened. His own legs stepped into the car, and he felt what might have been a soft, warm pad farther up his

37

back, and he was lowering himself into the back of the car and was seated looking ahead as if he had gotten into the car of his own free will.

"You're all under arrest," he said.

"That's nice," said Remo. "Hold this, will you, Chiun?" he said, and for a moment the sheriff felt the pad and pin prick on his spine release, and he almost crumpled. But then the identical feeling was there, and he was looking straight ahead again, not in control of his own body.

Remo skipped out of the car, telling Smith to follow, and he slid behind the wheel of the still running sheriff's car. He turned off the road and drove out into the flat scrub of the countryside, where the air was cleaner and where, far off, he saw a mesa. It was a good half-hour drive to that mesa, and when he stopped and Smith's car pulled up behind him, he saw the old man perspiring freely and breathing hard.

Smith must have noted Remo's expression because he said, "I'm all right."

"No, you're not," said Remo. "Push your head back and blow the air out of your lungs. Do it. Now."

Remo saw the lemony face look upward, the lips pucker, and the cheeks contract. He leaned into the car, and with a flat hand, pressed the last air out of the lungs. Smith's eyes went wide, his head popped forward in startled surprise, and then he settled down in the seat with a big smile. It was the first time Remo could remember him smiling that way. Probably the shock of the sudden relaxation.

"Ahhh," said Smith, sucking fresh air back deep into his lungs. Recovering his senses, the smile disappeared.

"All right, get on with it. I've got to get out of here as quickly as possible. I can't be connected with any incident like this," said Smith.

"Not publicly," said Remo.

"Not publicly, of course," said Smith.

"The emperor's eyes should never look upon the emperor's business," said Chiun, still holding the sheriff by the spine, like a ventriloquist with his hand in the back of a bigger than life-size dummy.

"I wouldn't mind seeing your techniques of questioning," said Smith.

"Unfortunately, they are a secret of Sinanju to be rented, but never sold," said Chiun.

When they got the sheriff out of view of the car, Chiun put him down on the ground, where the sheriff found himself still unable to move and listened in on a startling conversation.

The skinny white guy wanted to know why the Oriental had told someone else he wanted to go to some place named Sinny or something, and the old gook said the white guy should want to go, and the white guy said he never said he wanted to go because he had about all he could take of Sinny-joo right here in America, and the old gook said he was Sinny-joo, and he was going home, and if Remo wasn't good enough to want to go where he ought to go, then it wasn't the old gook's problem, and besides an emperor never wanted the truth anyway.

Was that middle-aged white man at the wheel some sort of emperor?

Then the pain began. But the sheriff found a way to control it. He could do it with his voice, by telling those fellas things. Like the happiness he had found. Yeah, he was a follower of the Blissful Master, but he didn't tell his friends because they would laugh at him. In fact, an archpriest of the Blissful Master's had told him it was better for all if very few knew. In the Blissful Master, he had found true peace and happiness, the kind he had been looking for all his life. And yes, well, he would kill for the Blissful Master because the Blissful Master was truth incarnate, the center of the universe in man. He was going to get the fellow who called himself Clete, but he found out that was done for him.

Suddenly the sheriff's skin was on fire, and even the words couldn't control it. No, he didn't know what any big plan was, just that there was something big going to happen, and every one of the followers was going to be happy forever and ever and ever. And, no, he wasn't sure of the arch-priest's name. But he could be reached at a storefront in San Diego, a small Divine Bliss Mission. Yes, he was sure he didn't know the name. The guy just phoned him once.

"Anything else you can think of?" came the voice from above.

"Nothing," said the sheriff, and then he went on his last bliss of a trip. Total relaxation. Lights out.

Remo stepped away from the body.

"He did not mention Sinanju," said Chiun. "But we do not have to let Smith know that."

"What are you angling for now?" asked Remo. "What did you tell Smith?"

"In the car, the emperor demanded to know about the ancient Sinanju records, and feeling loyalty to him, just as you do . . ."

"You don't feel loyalty."

"Feeling loyalty, just as you do, knowledge of the ancient records was forced out of me."

"Like wet out of a baby," said Remo.

"And I told Emperor Smith that we had records in Sinanju of the lineage of this Blissful Master creature, whoever he is."

"Just in case one lie didn't get you a free trip back home, another might."

"And Emperor Smith asked me if I remembered what the records said."

"And you couldn't, but if you got a good look again, it would all come back."

40

"I think that was it. Sometimes my memory fails me. You understand."

"I understand that first we're going to the San Diego mission."

There were mumblings in Korean about ingratitude and how only the most heartless of persons would deny a dying man a trip back home.

"You're dying, Little Father?" asked Remo, eyebrow cocked in an expression of suspicion.

"We're all dying," said Chiun. "Death is but the hand-maiden of life."

"I thought it was something like that," said Remo.

At the car, Smith was dozing; the parched face seemed truly relaxed.

"He's your man," Remo told him.

"Did you get a lead?"

"To Sinanju," said Chiun quickly.

"With a stop in San Diego," said Remo.

"Good," said Smith. "I guess we're most afraid of the unknown, and this thing frightens me because we don't know just what it is. You didn't get any indication of what was going to happen, did you?"

"Just something big."

"I believe we have read the prophecy of the ancient Blissful Masters," said Chiun. "It is not clear, but there was to come a time that a calamitous . . . let me see, a calamitous calamity was to be started, and it would come quickly once it was decided upon. That is what I remember. The rest of it is back in Sinanju."

"You know we might be able to airdrop you two directly into Sinanju by tomorrow," said Smith.

"The sub will do," said Remo. "After the stop in San Diego."

"Chiun knows about these things. You've got to listen to him," said Smith.

"And I know about Chiun. You've got to listen to me.

The Master of Sinanju knows what he chooses to know. And what he chooses not to know is sometimes more effective."

"I don't understand that," said Smith.

"Remo just pledged his loyalty thrice over," said Chiun, and now he was angered with his pupil. One did not tell emperors too much about one's real business.

CHAPTER FOUR

The Blissful Master, Maharaji Gupta Mahesh Dor, chosen by the force of the universe, born of that which had been born before and would be born again, heard the warnings from his priests and arch-priests. He listened from the golden pillow throne to this worry and that worry. Heard his women and his men tell of tales of this follower lost and that one killed. Heard, he did, of warnings from the east. Heard supplications that he delay, if only for a year, the big plan of which he sometimes spoke and which all knew would soon come to pass.

Women with heads shaved, and women with but the forelock left, and women with their hair full around their shoulders pressed their foreheads to the mosaic floors. Sweet incense rose from silver and ruby bowls. New flowers graced the mosaic ceiling.

And the Blissful Master spoke.

"Frankly, I don't need this shit. If you want to know where I'm at, that's where I'm at." His voice was squeaky fifteen, his round face glistened with sweat, his small mustache struggled hopelessly over a young brown lip.

"O Chosen One, O Perfect One, would that you

would not turn your perfect face from us. Would that you would consider our supplication," said a man with wizened brown face, an Ilhibad hill tribesman who had come down from the hills with his brothers to serve the father of the Blissful Master and who now served the son, for did not the son have the spirit of the father, and was not the spirit perfect, the way it would lead, the perfection it enjoyed, proof of the force itself that kept the community of faithful alive and fruitful and growing. And especially growing.

"Consider again," said the man.

"Consider. Consider. Consider," chanted the throng.

"All right, what's your name, let's hear it again," said Maharaji Dor to the brown man who was an arch-priest. The old buzzard had been around since Dor could remember, and he was tired of the dippy advice. "Go ahead, what's your name."

"Is it not written that there are three proofs of our truth?"

"Hey, sweetie, I run this lashup. You don't have to go back to basics with me. I'm the Blissful Master."

"First," said the arch-priest, his brown hands arching above his head, "is the proof of reality, of that which is. We are. That is proof number one."

"That's also a proof for Disneyland and the Taj Mahal," mumbled Dor to no one in particular. His eyes settled on the pale neck of the girl who had gotten that black Baptist, Powell, out here with her letter. Why was that man's name plaguing him? Of all the ministers he had seen here, of all the people he had met, that name stuck. He looked at the neck and remembered the Reverend Mr. Powell and, looking at the lines of the young thigh stretched against the pink sari, he thought it might be nice to bed again with what's her name.

"Proof two is that for generations we have always had a Blissful Master."

44

"Which would prove the Catholic Church more than it would us," mumbled the maharaji.

"And third, and final, absolute proof, we have grown, always grown. From a handful of the enlightened in your great grandfather's day, to more in your grandfather's day, to a large community in your father's day, and now to the worldwide enlightenment in your day. These are the proofs."

"Hail, Blissful Master. Hail him who brings peace and happiness, hail the truth in man's form," chanted the throng.

"All right, all right," said the maharaji.

"Thus we ask, lest wrong ideas about our growth cloud your truth, let us postpone your great plan for but a year until we are more secure from the negative forces," said the arch-priest.

"If we wait until all the negative forces are gone, we'll be sucking our thumbs here in Patna for another generation."

"But a follower has been killed in a disturbing way, a follower who carried arms."

"What was he doing with a gun? I assume it was a gun?"

"He was a sheriff. A man of one of the many governments in America. An enlightened one who had seen the true way."

"I'm sorry to hear that. We are deeply grieved that one of our true ones has suffered an ill fate physically. However, he has had in his life more happiness than those who have not been enlightened. Let us be thankful for his brief happiness. Next case."

"The manner in which he was killed causes alarm," persisted the arch-priest.

"You get alarmed at a change in the weather."

"His neck was shattered."

"He fell."

45

"In an American desert from which there was no great height."

"He tripped then," said the maharaji.

"The neck was shattered, not broken. Shattered by . . ."

"Enough," said the maharaji. "I'll see you alone." He clapped his hands and rose from his golden pillows. He left to the sounds of the heavy chanting with his arch-priest close behind him.

When they reached his game room, he noticed there was a new electronic device for him, called interplanetary. It was lit, and the little blips of light were dancing around the screen.

"All right. If I've told you once, I've told you a thousand times, not in front of the faithful. What are you telling them horror stories for?"

"But, O Perfect . . ."

"Shut up. Are we or are we not in the happiness business, yes or no?"

"But . . ."

"Yes or no?"

"Yes, we give the fulfillment of the happiness human beings were meant to have."

"So if we're happiness, why are you laying all these horror stories on the troops?"

"But we face danger."

The maharaji flipped a switch full throttle and sent a blip directly across the screen through weaving obstacles. A board above the screen lit up, signifying a win.

"If you go fast, you get through safely. If you go slowly . . ." The maharaji eased back on the throttle, and the blip immediately collided and was sent back to the right of the screen. The board above lit up a "crash."

"I have heard tales of men who can shatter a neck with their hands," said the arch-priest.

"Maybe they had a machine," said the maharaji.

"No machine. They saw only footprints around the body."

"So they did it with their hands. What's their price? We probably can get them cheaper than one of our ministers."

"They have not been found. I worry. For the men who could do this, I know, have been in India before, hundreds of years before, I believe in times before your great grandfather received his enlightenment. Our people were not always hill tribesmen. The Ilhibad once lived prosperously in the valleys. We served a great mogul, and one of our leaders thought, why should we who are the strength of the mogul, why should we who die for the mogul, why should we who are the foundation of the mogul, take crumbs from his table instead of filling our bellies on the sweetmeats?"

"You never get to the point, do you?" said the maharaji.

"And our ancestors planned that on the night of a great feast, they would slay the mogul and his sons and take his table and his women, his wealth and his power. But on that night our leader died. In a tent surrounded by faithful, he was found, his neck not only broken but shattered. And a new leader stepped forward and planned the assault on the mogul for the next night. But on the next night, he too was dead, his neck but skin covering jelly."

"C'mon, c'mon, get to the point."

"And a third leader . . ."

"Yeah, yeah, yeah. His neck too, right? So?"

"So the great mogul called the Ilhibad to his palace, and in ranks he stood us before him. And he told us that while we thought we were warriors, we were but babies with swords. And he called the best swordsman forward. And he called the best lancer forward. And he called the strongest-muscled of us forward. And he said to us that when the tiger is away, the monkey thinks he is king.

Here, he said, is a tiger. And before all, an Oriental appeared, a yellow man. And the mogul promised that if any of our best could slay this man, he could have the mogul's lands and women and table."

"And they didn't do it, so go on," said the maharaji.

"Ah, but how they failed. The swordsman's hands were severed. The lancer's eyes were plucked, and the back of the strong man was shattered, and so fast were the hands of this one Oriental that none of my ancestors could see them move. And then to each of the three dead men he went, and with a movement so slight it looked like a touch, he shattered their necks. And the mogul said that here was the tiger and that since we were monkeys, we should go where monkeys went. To the hills. Any man who stayed would have to face the Master. The mogul called this Oriental the Master. And he said that any of my ancestors who returned to the valley would have to face the Master. And that is the story, and not until this day, "O Perfection, have I heard of one who slays like that until our follower was killed in the state of New Mexico, America."

"So what's the problem?"

"The problem, O Perfection, is that on the day the black man of God died, the earth shook, and I now fear what comes from the east."

"You're afraid of some Chinaman, right?"

"Someone of the east."

"Tell me, what's your name, how did you ever get down from the mountain? I mean most of your people are still up there."

"I served your father, Precious One."

"Yeah, but why? I mean, why did you venture down?"

"Because your father freed me. He was the truth that freed me, and I and my many brothers, of all my people, ventured forth down from the mountains to Patna. We are the only Ilhibad who dare wear the silver mark on our foreheads while in the valley."

"Well, as good as my father was, I'm better. And if I'm not as good, then your proof is not as good. Therefore, get back to work and keep the Baptist ministers happy, okay?"

"My essence knows not to fear, but my stomach, O Perfection, does not heed my essence."

"You had a classy hit man who did the job on a whole tribe, so we'll buy us some hit men of our own. What's the grief or trouble? We'll get assassins to protect us from your stupid legend."

"I shall seek the assassins myself."

"You won't do anything of the kind. I wouldn't trust you and your brothers to chew gum right. I'll do it."

"But, Perfection, hiring killers is against the law in Western countries."

"It's against the law here too."

"But you know the laws of India are hopes, while those of those faraway places are mean and cruel rules, enforced whether a man be maharaji or untouchable."

And to his arch-priest, Maharaji Gupta Mahesh Dor gave this command:

"Get lost, and this time don't fuck up advance preparations. Kezar Stadium's a fortune to rent. And don't play with the Baptist ministers. You already killed one."

"We have others, O Blissful Master."

"Yeah, a crumby half dozen."

"Many of them proved difficult."

"Everything is difficult for an asshole."

"We have another who is dying, I regret to say."

"Shit," said the maharaji. "I have to do everything myself."

So he went down to the hospital and was allowed past barred doors by a bowing guard-priest and spoke in turn to each of the Baptist ministers. His words were brief, but always reassuring, that of course the ministers had done the right thing. Hadn't the god they worshipped made their bodies? Did their bodies lie to them? Did they think God wanted them to be unhappy? And besides, who had brought them here, but the will of their god?

To the minister who was dying, the Blissful Master asked why he did this to himself. Why did he not enjoy his life?

"Your way is death," gasped the man, his pale face haggard, his eyes red, his white hair matted on the hospital pillow. The maharaji dismissed the handmaidens waiting on the minister. He pulled back the pale gray blanket with Divine Bliss Mission, Inc., on it and saw the handcuffs and leg irons were still attached. The man had been here a week and was still in stage one. Dor knew that the human body could not stand stage one for a week. Already there were deep dark rings beneath the red eyes. He felt the chest with his fingertips. It was not a strong heartbeat.

"You're dying," said Dor.

"I know," said the man.

"Tell me, why did you resist your body? What made you do this foolish thing? The others did not resist."

"I know that."

"Why you?"

"I've been here before."

"In Patna?" asked Dor.

"No. Narcotics. I was a pimp once. I was a gambler. I was a burglar, a whorer, a murderer, and a thief. The lowest of the low. And I know a fix when I get one. I've turned girls out onto the street like that. The sex and the fix and they're yours, and the longer they stay, the stronger the habit of staying gets, and then you don't even need the fix."

"I didn't know it was so common. That's interesting. I

50

thought it was a formula invented by my great grand-father."

"The devil is not new."

"Yes, but the combination. The withdrawal of a person's sense and the substitution of the senses you want."

"Old hat."

"But this drug isn't heroin. We use a symphony of drugs along with the talk."

"Heroin, booze, pot, even a cigarette if a person wants it badly enough. Anything will do. Food will do if your man's hungry enough. Old hat, buddy."

"Then why didn't you go along?"

"Jesus."

"That's old hat," said the maharaji.

"He is new, and I will see him fresh."

The young man rubbed his moon face and thought, then said, very slowly and very carefully:

"Do you know we bring peace of mind to thousands? And without drugs too? Thousands. Drugs are just for special cases—that we need something special from."

"You bring false peace."

"You reformed scumbags are impossible to deal with," said the maharaji.

"Praised be the Lord."

"Thank you," said Dor absent-mindedly and then realized the man wasn't talking to him.

"Tell you what," said the Blissful Master. "I think I can save your body. Let's make a deal."

"No deal," said the man. Both eyes began to twitch. Dor knew the end was near now.

"I'll give you whatever you want if you can recommend a hit man to me."

"A what?"

"A professional killer."

"No, I am gone from that life. I don't deal with those people."

51

"I'll tell you what. I've got five other Baptist ministers here. Five. I'll let one go if you give me the name of a good killer. I mean good. Most people are incompetent. Give me the name of a competent one, and I'll give you back one of your people to your god. How about it? A guaranteed Christian for you, against the life of some target who's most likely a heathen. Maybe even a Catholic or a Jew. You hate them, don't you?"

"No."

"I thought all you people hated each other."

"No."

"If there's one thing that abounds, it's misinformation. What about it? I'll give two. I'll be down to three Baptists then. You can't leave me with any less."

"All of them."

"All right. All of them."

"Release all of them from your evil ways, and I will, God forgive me, give you the name of a hired killer."

"Done. You have my word on everything that's sacred to me. The word of the Maharaji Gupta Mahesh Dor, the perfection on earth, the Blissful Master. My secret bond. Where can I reach the guy?"

The dying minister told of a river called the Mississippi. Up that river from New Orleans were many towns. Some were settled by the French. In one of those towns was a family named De Chef, although they used the name Hunt now. From father to son, this family had passed on its methods. They were the finest marksmen in the world. But this was twenty-five years ago. He did not know if they were still in business.

"Once in the rackets, always in the rackets," said the maharaji. "What's the name again?"

"De Chef or Hunt."

"How far upriver from New Orleans? I said, how far?"

Dor placed his hand on the man's chest. He could not feel the heartbeat. He put his ear to the pasty flesh, which felt cool. Nothing. He quickly lunged to the foot of the bed and grabbed the minister's chart, which was an unbroken line going down. There was a ballpoint pen attached to the clipboard. In a rush he wrote down the name. De Chef.

He ripped the sheet from the chart and walked to the door. In the corridor outside was one of the former Baptist ministers.

"O Blissful Master, I heard your promise to send me back to my former ways. Please don't do this. I have found truth here."

"What makes you think I would kick you out?"

"Because of the promise you made to the unenlightened one."

"Oh, to the stiff. In the room back there, right?"

"Yes. You promised by everything sacred to you."

"I'm sacred to me. You're sacred to me. We are sacred to us. That rotting carrion back in the room was unenlightened, and therefore he is not sacred. One does not desecrate sanctity by bonding it to the profane. Therefore there was never a bond in the first place."

"Praised be your eternal truth," said the man, and he covered Dor's feet with kisses. Which was hard because the Blissful Master was walking at the time. Very quickly. You had to keep a good pace or they'd get your instep all sloshed up with saliva.

"What do we have in New Orleans?" asked the Blissful Master of one of his arch-priests. "We got to have a mission there. It's a major market area. I know it."

CHAPTER FIVE

The Divine Bliss Mission on Lorky Street in San Diego stood like a fresh-washed face in a lineup of bums. Its windows were sparkling clear, its walls white with fresh paint. Around it, crumbling clapboard houses settled into their dry wooden frames, gray wood exposed like nude corpses waiting for the grave. Grass grew on Lorky Street, the last surviving remnants of what had been lawns before the neighborhood had fallen prey to a government housing policy of helping people to buy homes with no money down and with no prospect of keeping up the monthly payments. The "buyers" had lived in the houses a year or less, let them decay, then skipped on the unpaid mortgage bills, and the decayed houses stayed empty. And decayed more.

Remo looked at the street in the afternoon sunlight and sighed.

"I shipped out to Vietnam from this city. I went with a girl who lived on this street. I remember this street. It was beautiful once. I thought I was fighting so that someday I would own a home on this street. Or on one like it. I used to think a lot of things."

"A girl would go out with you the way you looked before I found you?" asked Chiun.

"I used to be a good-looking guy."

"To whom?"

"Girls," said Remo.

"Oh," said Chiun.

"Why do you ask?"

"I was just wondering what Americans found attractive. I must tell this to Sinanju when we return. That is Smith's promise, and you cannot break the promise of an emperor."

"You never told me that. You always told me that what an emperor did not know about you was always in your best interest."

"Unless," said Chiun, "it is a decree. Smith has decreed that we will go to Sinanju."

"We're going to board the sub by tomorrow morning. I promise. I just want to clear up a couple of things. Before we go to Patna, I'd like to find out if I can settle this thing right here in the states."

"And what if it takes days and weeks?" asked Chiun. "I go without my luggage, without my special set that makes pictures. I go like a wanderer."

"Your fourteen steamer trunks and your television set are on board the sub."

"Aha, but until we are aboard the submarine, I am without those necessities that make life less burdensome for a weary man who longs for his home. It has been many years."

"Since when are you weary?"

"It is always tiring attempting to enlighten the invincibly ignorant. Do not be proud of your triumph."

A coughing roar of motorcycles intruded down the street and a phalanx of black cyclists with skulls painted on their silver jackets turned the corner of Lorky and drove imperiously in front of Remo and Chiun. Ordi-

56

narily, this would have been a simple brushback with an old man struggling to jump for his life and the younger man tripping over his own feet. The Black Skulls could do this well. They called it "slicing Whitey," and a week did not go by without one of the group getting his bones, which really meant encouraging some white to jump in such a way that he broke an arm or a leg in the fall. You could always get your bones with the older whites because they were more brittle than the younger ones.

The Black Skulls were getting many bones this summer because of a new policy of police community relations under which, instead of arresting the cyclists for assault, they were called in to discuss white racism and how the San Diego Police Department could overcome it. Invariably, the prescription was, "Stop hassling us, man."

Thus, unhassled by police, the Black Skulls made many bones that summer, although not in Italian neighborhoods whose unenlightened racial policies led the Black Skulls to a unanimous decision that "You don't mess with the guineas." Sometimes, the Black Skulls would work on black but only when the day had been unfruitful of white victims.

This day, the last cyclist looked back to see if he got both the old man with the beard and the funny yellow robe, and the white dude with the gray slacks and blue turtleneck sweater. They seemed unbothered, so Willie "Sweetman" Johnson and Muhammid Crenshaw signaled the pack to wheel around and make another pass.

This time Willie "Sweetman" Johnson, who had been called a failure of the San Diego school system—his last teacher had failed to teach him to read, possibly because she was being raped at the time by Sweetman himself and the alphabet came unclear through her bloody and battered lips—this time, Sweetman chose a closer path. Like right through the hips of the younger honkey. And he missed. The honkey was there in front of the built-up

57

chrome bar on top of the front wheel guard, and then the honkey was not there.

"You see that boy move?" asked Sweetman, whirling around at the other end of the street.

"Ah hits da yella one," said Muhammid Crenshaw. "But he still dere."

"This time they go," yelled Sweetman.

"For the love of Allah," yelled Muhammid Crenshaw.

"Yeah, for motherfuckin' Allah," yelled Sweetman, and the four cyclists closed on the two figures.

Remo saw the cyclists wheel for a return run.

"I'll tell you the truth, Little Father. I want to see Sinanju too. I know I'm the best pupil you ever had, and I want to see the young men of Sinanju."

"You have become adequate because I have been willing to spend extra time with you," said Chiun.

"Doesn't matter," Remo said. "I'm still the best you've had. Me. Whitey. Paleface. Me."

And with a simple backhand snap, Remo took the first rider off his cycle and held him. Chiun was a bit more efficient. He let his cyclist continue with a minor alteration in the plastic shield over his face mask. There was a small hole in it the width of a forefinger. There was also a small hole in the forehead behind the mask. It oozed red as the driver, not caring anymore, zoomed complacently into a fire hydrant, where he became separated from his machine and sailed off into a pile of rotting garbage, with which he blended very well.

Remo's rider kicked and screamed. Remo held him by the neck. Sweetman tried to reach the rod in his jacket pocket. Unfortunately, Sweetman was now unqualified for holding a gun. His right arm ended in a bloody wrist.

The other two riders, assuming Muhammid Crenshaw, now lying with the rest of the garbage, had hit a bump and missteered, and not sure whether Sweetman had gotten off his wheels to deal personally with the honkey or

58

had been yanked off, wheeled back at the two in the middle of the street.

Remo slipped down to Sweetman's ankles, where, grabbing both, he swung the flailing leather-jacketed man in a nice, smooth horizontal path that caught the brace of oncoming cyclists full face. Chiun refused to move or even recognize Remo. He wanted no part of a person who had such arrogance as to believe he was a good pupil.

Sweetman took the other cyclists off their wheels with a nice crack.

"Home run," said Remo, but Chiun refused to look. Sweetman's helmet went skittering across the gutter. One cyclist lay flattened, the other rose groggily to his knees. One cycle dizzily circled the street and ended in an abandoned doorway. The other tumbled and stopped nearby, its gas tank spilling fumes and dark liquid in the gutter. Remo saw his human bat had a wild Afro, a cone twice the size of the helmet.

"Hi," said Remo, looking down at the Afro. "My name is Remo. What's yours?"

"Mufu," said Sweetman.

"Mufu, who sent you?"

"No one send me, man. Get yo mufu hands off'n me. Ah rack yo ass."

"Let's play school," said Remo. "I ask you a question, and you give me a positive answer with a sweet cheerful smile. All righty?"

"Mufu."

Remo walked the cyclist upside down to the spilling gas tank, where he dipped the Afro into the liquid, sloshing the head around. Then he walked his charge back to the cyclist getting to his feet.

"Got a light?" said Remo.

He saw a switchblade knife come out of the jacket and with his toe kicked it away.

"Three points," said Remo, who was in a scoring mood.

59

"Field goal." And with the same foot coming back on its heel, he shattered an ear drum. "That's for not listening," said Remo. "I want a light."

"Don't give da man no match. My fro's been gasolined."

"Fu yu mufu," said the cyclist with the bleeding ear.

"You talking to me?" said Remo.

"No, to de nigger, Sweetman," said the cyclist, and he struck a match.

Remo lifted Sweetman higher. The hair caught like a torch, burning up to the eyebrows.

"Who sent you?" asked Remo.

"A as in apple, B as in boy, C as in cat," cried Sweetman.

"What's he talking about?" asked Remo.

"School. He learning de alphabet to get his degree from de teacher's college. He din wan take no easy course like Afro studies. You don't have to count fo that. Or spell or know de alphabet."

"Arghhh," cried Sweetman as his brain stopped working. Which was just as well. He had never gotten past F as in fly, even in his senior year in high school.

Remo dropped the legs.

"And you, my friend, who sent you?"

"No one send us. We do it for fun."

"You mean you'd kill somebody and not get paid for it?"

"We just funning."

"Your funning interfered with my conversation. Do you know that?"

"Ah sorry."

"Sorry isn't enough. You don't go interfering with people's conversations in the middle of the street. It's not nice."

"Ah be nice."

"See that you do. Get your friends out of here."

60

"They dead."

"Well, bury them or something," said Remo, and he stepped over the charred head of the writhing body and joined Chiun on the sidewalk.

"Sloppy," said Chiun.

"I was in the street. I worked with what I had."

"Sloppy, careless, and messy."

"I just wanted to be sure they weren't part of the Divine Bliss Mission."

"Of course. Play in the streets. Visit holy houses. Anything but taking your benefactor to his home. Even your emperor orders it, but, no, you must play your games. And why, I asked myself, must someone to whom I have given so much, refuse me a simple visit to my birthplace. Why I asked myself. Why? Where have I gone wrong in his education? Is it possible that I am at fault?"

"I can't wait to hear the answer," said Remo. The door was heavy wood with a small glass circle in the center of it. Remo knocked.

"Was I at fault, I asked myself. And being scathingly honest, I came to the conclusion, that, no, everything I gave you was perfect and right. I had performed miracles with you. This I admitted to myself. Then why does my pupil still do improper things? Why does my pupil still deny me a simple little favor? In being harsh with myself, sparing no criticism, I was forced to the following conclusion. Remo, you are cruel. You have a cruel streak."

"You really know how to tear yourself down, Little Father," said Remo.

An eye appeared in the glass hole, and the door opened.

"Quickly, inside," said a young girl with a grace of freckles under her pink scarf. The scarf blended into a light, clear robe. A silver line was painted on her forehead. Chiun noted the silver line carefully, but said nothing.

"Quickly, the cyclists are out again."

"The guys in the jackets?" said Remo.

61

"Yes."

"You don't have to worry about them." Remo pointed to the last cyclist stacking his comrades against the curb.

"All praised be the Blissful Master. He has shown us the way. Come everyone, look at our deliverance." Faces crowded around the young girl, some with silver lines, some without. Chiun looked at every silver line.

"The Blissful Master will always show the way," the girl said. "Let the doubting hearts be stilled."

"The Blissful Master didn't do it. I did it," said Remo.

"You worked through his will. You were only the instrument. Praised be the Blissful Master. His truth is manifest. Oh, there were doubters when we bought this house. There were doubters who said this neighborhood was unsafe. But the Blissful Master said we should get an abode that fit our purse, mindless of where it was. And he was right. He was always right. He has always been right and will always be right."

"Can we come in?" asked Remo.

"Enter. You have been sent by the Blissful Master."

"I was thinking of joining you," said Remo. "I came to find what you're about. You have an arch-priest for this place, don't you?"

"I am the arch-priest of the San Diego Mission," came a voice from up a stairwell. "You are the men who made the street safe, correct?"

"Correct," said Remo.

"I will see you and make the way ready for you if you will but rise above your doubts."

"We will be starting an introductory lesson soon," said the girl.

"They will have a private introduction. They have earned it," said the voice.

"As you will it," said the girl, and she bowed.

Remo and Chiun climbed the stairs. A man whose face was a remnant of a losing fight against long-ago acne

62

greeted them with a short bow. He too wore a pink robe. Remo could see his hair had been shaved from the front of his head. He wore sandals and smelled as if he had been dipped in incense.

"I am a priest. I have been to Patna, there to gaze with my own eyes upon perfection. There is perfection on earth, but the Western mind rebels against it. Your very act of coming here shows you recognize the rebellion within you. I ask a question: What happens in rebellion?"

Chiun did not answer; he was staring at the silver streak down the priest's forehead. Remo shrugged. "You got me," he said.

They followed the priest into a room that had a dome of pink plaster material. In the center of the dome hung a golden chain, and at the end of the chain was a four-sided picture of a fat-faced young Indian boy working on his first mustache.

Pillows were stacked against the corner. A deep-piled rug of intricate red and yellow designs covered the floor. The priest continued:

"What happens in rebellion is two parts, at least two parts set in opposition. They harm each other. Every person who does not believe he can be unified within himself, who fights against his passions, is in rebellion. Why do you think you have passions?"

"Because he is white like you," said Chiun. "Everyone knows whites can't control their passions and are invincibly cruel at heart, especially to their benefactors."

"All people have the same passions," said the pock-faced priest, sitting down beneath the picture of the fat-faced kid. "All men, but for one, are alike."

"River garbage," said Chiun. "White Western river garbage."

"Why do you come here, then?" asked the priest.

"I am here because I am here. That is the true unity before you now," said Chiun.

63

"Ah," said the priest. "You understand then."

"I understand the tides are favorable in the harbor of San Diego, but that it is very difficult to launch a submarine here on the second floor of this building."

"Talk to me," said Remo. "I'm the one who came to join."

"We are all made perfect," said the priest, "but we have been taught imperfection."

"If that were the case," said Chiun, "babies would be the wisest among us. Yet they are the most helpless among us."

"They are taught wrong things," said the priest.

"They are taught to survive. Some are taught better than others. They are not taught ignorance as you contend. And these passions you talk of as so holy are merely the basic thrusts of survival. A man taking a woman is survival of the group. A person eating is survival of the body. A person afraid is survival of the person. Passions are the first level of survival. The mind is the higher level. Discipline, properly pursued, brings together all rebellion into perfection. It is long, it is hard, and when doing it properly, learning it properly, man feels small and inadequate. That is how we grow. There has never been a shortcut to anything worthwhile." Thus spoke the Master of Sinanju, in truth, even as he looked at the silver marking.

Remo looked at Chiun and blinked. He had heard this before and had been taught it during many years. He knew it as well as he knew his being. What surprised him was that Chiun would bother explaining these things to a stranger.

"I see surprise upon your face," Chiun said to Remo. "I say these things for your benefit. Just so you do not forget."

"You must think I'm pretty dippy, Little Father."

"I know passage to Sinanju waits for us in the harbor,

and we are sitting here with this." A graceful hand opened toward the priest, who sighed.

"Your way is the pain and inches and small costly victories over your own body," said the priest. "Mine is the immediate true enlightenment that even your own bodies will verify. We have three proofs first. One, the Blissful Master exists, therefore he is. He is reality. We do not ask you to accept anything that is not reality. Two, he, through his ancestors, has existed for many years. Therefore it is not just one of myriad passing realities. And, third, and finally, he grows. Like the infinite universe, we expand each day and each year. These then are the three proofs."

"They'd work just as well for air pollution," said Remo. Chiun was silent. There was no more need to banter words with the robed one.

"There is a pool of eternal and original force that your mind has been clouded from. This is because of your improper teachings. We simply, through the perfection of the Blissful Master, return you to that pool, show you the way to realize the truth about yourself. First. Close your eyes. Close them. Tightly. Good. You see little white lights. Those are the infinite lights in fragments. You have robbed yourself of the pure stream of life. I will give you the pure stream of life."

Remo felt fingertips press against his closed eyelids. He could feel the priest's heavy breathing above him. Smell the meat on his breath. Smell the sweat of his struggling body. The small globules of light that all people see when they close their eyes quickly and then look behind their eyelids, became a pure and relaxing line of light, unbroken and restful. It would have been very impressive, had not Chiun shown him something similar and more restful many years before, a simple exercise that was taught to children in Sinanju who were unable to nap properly.

"Wonderful," said Remo.

"Now that we have given you some power of release, we give you more. Say to yourself, 'my mind is at peace, my body is at rest.' Say it with me. My mind is at peace, my body is at rest. Feel yourself become one with the light. You are the light. You are pure. Everything that comes to you and from you is pure. You are good. You are good. Everything about you is good."

Remo heard very light footsteps enter the room. A soft linen quietly touched the carpeted floor. Another set of feet. More linen. Normal hearing would not have picked it up. The priest was setting them up for a surprise.

"Open your eyes," said the priest. "Open."

Two girls stood before them, naked, smiling. On the right, a mulatto, on the left a blonde, more blond on her head than elsewhere. Their only garments were silver lines painted down their foreheads.

"Americans," said Chiun. "Typical Americans."

"Do you think that is wrong? Do you think the body is wrong?"

"For Americans it is just fine," said Chiun. "How grateful I am that you have not infected Korea with your ways."

"Biggest whores in the world come from Korea, Little Father. You told me that yourself."

"From Pyongyang and Seoul. Not from decent places like Sinanju."

"Whore is a word that pollutes a thing that is good," said the priest. He clapped his hands and the two girls walked before Remo and Chiun. They lowered themselves to their knees. The blonde slipped off Remo's loafers. The mulatto tried to get beneath Chiun's robes, but the longer fingernails were always where her fingers were, darting to the palms of her hands, touching her fingertips, and pushing so that in face-twisted frustration she was forced to withdraw her hands and shake them out.

66

"They feel as if they've been in an ant's nest," she said.

"It is all right," said the priest. "Some cannot be helped. It happens to the old . . ."

Chiun looked around the room confused. Where was the old person this priest talked of?

The blonde took off Remo's socks and kissed the soles of his feet.

"Is that bad?" asked the priest. "Have you been taught that that is evil?"

The blonde brought her body closer to the feet and rubbed her breasts against Remo's soles. He could feel her getting excited. With his toes, he unexcited her, and with a squeak, she blinked out of her passion.

"Perhaps you prefer boys," said the priest.

"Girls are fine. I just don't have all that much time. I wish to join."

"Even before the body enlightenment?"

"Yeah."

"There are forms, you know. We provide you all your wealth and sustenance. You no longer have to worry about where your next meal will come from or what you have to eat. We provide all. In return, you must divest yourself of all your worldly goods."

"I'm wearing my worldly goods," said Remo.

"He has what you can never have," Chiun said to the priest. "What you can never take from him. The only true possession that lasts. What he knows in his mind and his body. And being unable to understand what he understands, you can never take it from him."

"Ah, so you think I'm pretty good, Little Father," said Remo.

"I am thinking you are not so low as this rut-faced pig's ear."

"Invincibly ignorant," said the priest to Remo. "I'm

afraid your father, he is your father, isn't he, you call him father, I'm afraid there is nothing I can do for him."

"The worm never helps the eagle," said Chiun.

"I am but a new priest. We have priests who would, with their hands, turn you into molasses so that you would beg for mercy. They come from the Vindhya Mountains."

"Do they have the silver mark on their heads, like you and the girls?" asked Chiun.

"Yes. That is the mark of honor among the followers of the Blissful Master who have been to Patna. And those priests are most fearsome. They would teach you the error of your ways."

"When did they leave the mountains?" asked Chiun.

"When the grandfather of the Blissful Master told them to come. It was another proof of his perfection, his coming and his truth."

"They just left those mountains as free as you please?" asked Chiun.

"With singing hearts."

"Without even a caution?" asked Chiun.

"With praise for the Blissful Master."

"Just because he said they could leave, they just walked down into the valley? Into Patna? Out in the open?"

"Yes."

"Who is your Blissful Master that he would tell anyone they could go anywhere they wish? Who is he? How dare he?"

"He is perfection."

"You are faulty of mind and face," said Chiun. "Bad news he has given us, Remo. Bad news."

"What is it, Little Father?"

"I will tell you later. First settle your business with this roach. Ah, it is sad. An assassin's work is never done."

Remo talked to the priest. As a recent convert to the wisdom of the Blissful Master, Remo explained he had

68

come to hear the truth. And since priests always told the truth, Remo wanted to know the truth about the upcoming event. The big one.

"Ah, the big one. It will be the biggest," said the priest. He clapped his hands, and the girls put on their robes and left, the blonde casting a betrayed look at Remo.

"I saw what you did in the street out there to the gang of toughs," said the priest. "Even if you have no wealth, we can use your services. We have many people who just give services. We have them in high and important places. We have them in the middle ages and the young ages. You would be surprised to learn who is with us."

"Try me," said Remo.

"That is secret."

"No, it's not," said Remo, and he was proven right for with a face squinting in pain, the priest told of all the important people he knew who belonged secretly to the Blissful Master, and Remo remembered every name. There were others too, the priest said, but he did not know their names. Honest and don't hurt me anymore, I don't know their names, he told Remo. Nor did he know the exact nature of the big event about to happen, but the Blissful Master was coming to Kezar Stadium in San Francisco.

Remo said he thought he might have been too harsh. He was going to be reasonable. He would reason with the priest.

"If you don't tell me exactly what's going to happen at that stadium, I'm reasonably going to separate your head from your shoulders."

"I don't know. I don't know. I swear to God, I don't know."

"Which God?"

"The real one."

Chiun stepped between them, and with hands moving

like the flutter of butterflies, dispatched the priest on the neck.

"He does not know. Do not waste your time. We have work to do."

"You didn't let me finish with him. I told you we'd go to Sinanju afterward. I have my job to do also."

"We are not going to Sinanju. That is the sad news. I have other work to do. Older work. Indians have memories like sieves. In four hundred years, they forget everything. Everything. We must delay our return to Sinanju, jewel of the West Korean Bay, pearl of cities, vessel of beauty."

"What about the sub?"

"It can wait. Your country has many ships. There is but one Master of Sinanju, and he must sustain true and previous agreements."

CHAPTER SIX

When Remo gave the names he had learned of top followers of the Blissful Master to Smith on a closed line at 6:15 p.m., he heard a long silence and thought that the automatic cutoff had been triggered by some eavesdropping device. Then Smith spoke.

"A few of those people are highly sensitive. More than a few, Remo. Are there any chances that converts can be deprogrammed?"

"How should I know?" said Remo.

"You went through their program, didn't you?"

"So?"

"Perhaps in going through the program and not succumbing, you might have some ideas about how some highly sensitive personnel could be deprogrammed."

"Drop them from the Empire State Building."

"Thank you very much," said Smith.

"I need passports for India."

"You think that's your best chance of getting at this thing?"

"I guess."

"What does that mean?"

"Chiun thinks so. For some reason, he's willing to give up going home for it."

"Any word on the big event?"

"Nothing more. Just Kezar Stadium."

"With a few of those converts, if they can't be deprogrammed, they're going to have to be . . . er . . . retired."

"I told you the Empire State Building."

"I'm beginning to wonder whether you do have a cruel streak."

"You've been talking to Chiun."

"I've been counting bodies."

"If you want me to live in peace with the rest of mankind, just say the word, Smitty."

"Your passports will be at your hotel."

On the flight to Calcutta, Remo heard Chiun mumble something about faulty memories and some people needing reminders. The stewardess asked how they wished their dinner, and Chiun answered in a language Remo had never heard. Chiun explained it was Oriya and that the stewardess was obviously from the people who spoke that language because of the way she wrapped her sari.

Chiun pointed out that while the crew might call itself Indian, they were really of many different peoples, none of whom had any respect for each other, much less affection. He said it was only whites in America who worried about Indians starving. The different peoples of India were always unconcerned when ill befell others, and since the starving ones were never in government, the government did not really care.

"When they come to you for food again, you should let them eat their atomic bombs. You fill their bellies to give them the leisure time to call you names, and they use their own money to build bombs. I can understand the Indians. They are venal and vile and have always been and will always be. Know this about India and its people, if you know nothing else. It is the white men who put the thoughts of brotherhood on their tongues, and it has never reached their hearts."

"What about Mahatma Gandhi?" said Remo.

"What about Remo Williams? Would you say Americans have body discipline because of one person? No. The Indians, I can understand. What I do not understand is why you have taken it upon yourself to feed the mouths they would not feed themselves."

"I'm not feeding anybody."

"Your country. Your country feeds people who break promises," said Chiun and would speak no more.

The customs man at Delhi noticed that the series of passports that Remo and Chiun used was often used by the CIA. He also noticed that the two had no luggage.

"India will not suffer imperialistic intrusion within her bosom," the customs man said.

"Ten rupees," said Remo.

"But India will always welcome her friends," said the customs man. "And don't pay more than two rupees for any Indian woman. You can buy one for eight. Complete. Own her. Use her for fertilizer when you're tired of her. What is the purpose of your visit?"

"Enlightenment from the Blissful Master at Patna."

"You can get enlightenment here in Delhi. What sort of enlightenment are you chaps looking for?"

"The Blissful Master."

"He's been doing a bangup business lately," said the customs man. "Bangup."

Transportation to Patna was an old Packard that apparently hadn't been tuned since it left the states. Remo knew Chiun was still bothered about something because he spoke little during the two days' journey. When the driver held out his hand for payment, Chiun muttered something about faulty memories and slapped the hand away. When Remo started peeling off some bills, Chiun forbade it.

The driver jumped out of the car and began yelling. People with dusty feet and tired brown faces formed behind the driver. They became a crowd. The driver, encouraged by his support, changed his shouting into a harangue. Chiun translated:

"He says we have come to steal food from his mouth. He says foreigners still think they can do anything in India they want. He says we have much money on us, and it would serve us right if he took all of it, sharing it with his new-found friends. Have you heard enough, Remo?"

"Yes," said Remo.

"Good," said Chiun, and with barely a flick of his right wrist, he dropped the man in the dust of the streets of Patna. The new Indian Coalition of Patna vanished in the dust and hot sun. The man was alone, his 1947 Packard chugging in neutral, his cares behind him.

Chiun pointed to a large white cement wall with wooden doors.

"There," he said.

"How do you know?" asked Remo.

"Do you see those carvings in the wooden door?"

"Like the silver lines on the foreheads?"

"Correct. It means this house or palace, or if it is on a person, that person, is protected by a certain tribe, the Ilhibad."

"I see," said Remo.

"That is a lie. They can protect no one in the valley and they know it."

Chiun marched to the high wooden door. His white fringed head barely touched the lowest heavy metal bolt on the door.

"Hear ye, hear ye, O you worms of the mountainside. A Master of Sinanju has come to remind you of your word to a master of our house that you would stay in the

74

mountains to which he banished you. Oh, you vile bugs, fluttering in your trepidation."

With a short flat slap at the wood, Chiun produced a booming thud.

"Come out, I wish to remind you of your promise. Come, wriggling worms."

He turned from the door and smiled. He nodded for Remo to follow. "Sometimes I'm eloquent," he said. "They will now all cluster at that door with their weapons, bodies giving other bodies courage. They will not have enough courage to open the door, just to stand there. I know these people. I was taught of them as a small boy, just as I try to teach you. Fortunately, I was a good pupil. I have not been as fortunate in my pupils as my instructor was."

The wall butted into a large outcropping, and they climbed. Not like other climbers did they climb, but with a steady moving upward as if going along on a level. At the top of the wall, they saw a turbaned head. It was looking toward the courtyard. They could smell the fragrant aromas of spicy stews cooking in the kitchens of the Blissful Master's Palace. Chiun smiled at Remo once more as they ascended the wall. The turbaned one held a submachine gun at the ready, but it was pointing down into the courtyard, where a cluster of other turbaned men crouched, their weapons at the ready, all pointing to the door.

"See. I know them. I know their minds," said Chiun. The wall guard turned, startled to hear a voice, and when he saw Chiun, his mouth opened, and he shrieked.

"Eeyah." His pink robes spread moisture at his loins, and the gun shook in his hands.

Remo saw the finger tighten on the trigger, but the awesome hands of the Master of Sinanju had the turban and were unraveling it. Then, with a looping snap, they made it a noose around the neck, and with this noose, spun the guard in two slow circles, releasing him in an arc down into the courtyard.

Into a window beneath a large golden dome Chiun moved, with Remo following. Pinging bullets picked outside at the thick wall as they moved from window to window. Then the bullets stopped, and it was so quiet Remo could almost hear Chiun's footsteps on the tile floors. Remo looked down into the courtyard. The tribesmen were conferring.

Chiun moved to the center of a high window and stood there with arms folded.

"Watch this," said Chiun. "I knew it would be such."

One man knelt over the twisted body of the guard who had been on the wall. He examined the neck.

"Are you the one?" called out the man kneeling over the body.

"If I come down to where you crawl, O worm of the mountain, I will show you I am the one."

The men conferred again with arms waving, voices chopping at one another.

Remo couldn't see a decision being made, but obviously they had reached a conclusion. It was not so much a run to the door as a scramble. Men couldn't run in a crowd. They clawed and banged at the gate and grabbed for the bars, and like ants assaulting a huge, dark vertical crumb, they managed to move one giant door out into the street of Patna. Through this door they ran, some with weapons, some without.

"Where are they going?" asked Remo.

"Home. Where they belong. And where they will stay this time. Now we can go to Sinanju. I did not wish to return home, leaving untidiness out in the world. I must confess, if the previous Master had done his job properly, none of this would have been necessary. But we will not discuss that. Done is done and rightly done, it is forever."

"This an old contract for a hit or something?"

"You demean the assassin's art. You Americanize it."

"Yeah, yeah. I've got business too. We are employed by Smith, and an emperor's command, as you recently said, is holy."

"When it is a proper command. Emperors can be the most dangerous and impossible of all people because their artificial power deprives them of the constraints normal men use to make their way properly in the world."

But Remo was not listening. He was down the hall, moving from room to room. The chambers were deserted. The large rooms were deserted. The kitchens were deserted but for pots bubbling on wood fires. The palace had central air conditioning but old wood-burning fires. There was indirect lighting but windows made of blown glass, as if modern machinery was yet to be. There was incense in sticks and triangular cubes, all with the bumps of the handmade process. And then there was the computer room. Did nothing run without computers nowadays? He found cells, some with dried blood on leg shackles. There was a hospital. Old brass beds and modern cardiovascular devices. There was a bump under a blanket in one bed, and Remo could smell its condition. The sweet, nauseating smell of the long-dead filled his nostrils, and if he stayed longer it would, as the stench of death always did, fill his clothes. It was the smell that didn't wear off you right away.

Remo pulled back the sheets. A middle-aged Caucasian, about five-feet-ten, dead at least a day. The corpse had released its bowels and had begun to swell. The skin had burst around the handcuffs. A brown blood-dried cross had been drawn near the right hand, which was now a caked pink and brown ball. On the floor, Remo found a gold emblem with a silver stripe on it, and pocketed it.

Remo resumed breathing when he left the room. Down the hall he heard crying. In an alcove with the picture of the fat-faced kid surrounded by flowers, a blonde girl sobbed into her cupped hands.

"Who are you?" asked Remo.

"I am one who was not worthy to accompany the Blissful Master. My life is shattered fragments. Oh, blissful, blissful, Blissful Master."

"Where'd he go?"

"Left for glory."

"Let's try this again, honey. What is your name? First and last. And specifically, what place did the Blissful Master go to?"

"Joleen Snowy. He went to America."

"Good. Where in America?"

"To Kezar Stadium."

"Which seat?" said Remo, who felt he was getting lucky.

"No seat. He will be the center of it. It's the big thing that's coming."

"Beautiful. What big thing?"

"The third proof of his truth."

"Which is what?"

"That he grows."

"What's he going to do when he grows?"

"Prove he is in truth the truth."

"And we were doing so well too," said Remo.

"Oh, where will I find another master?" sobbed Joleen.

Down the corridor, a bowl cupped in his hands, came Chiun, the Master of Sinanju, and Remo thought of ways to tell him he would not be going home right away. He would have to be diplomatic.

"What's in the bowl, Little Father?"

"My first good meal since I was home."

"Better enjoy it," said Remo diplomatically. "You're not getting another for a long time."

CHAPTER SEVEN

Ferdinand De Chef Hunt crumpled the paper from his mid-morning Danish and flipped it over his left shoulder into a wastepaper basket three desks behind him. He knew it always gave his co-workers a little thrill to see a man know where something was without looking. Anything to distract the other analysts from the big board at the end of the room that blinked out the baleful truth about activity on the New York Stock Exchange.

As the stocks had plummeted, Hunt, a drug industry specialist and customers' man, in the New Orleans office of Dalton, Harrow, Petersen and Smith, member New York Stock Exchange, had found himself finding new euphemisms for the word "depression." The market was fluttering before flight, the market was experiencing a technical adjustment, the market was building a lower foundation for a more solid climb.

Into the second year of this depression, while government officials were debating whether the country was headed for a "recession," Ferdinand De Chef Hunt tried little levities when asked his opinion on the drug market.

"Take them intravenously," he would say.

"Heh, heh," his customers would say and somehow didn't phone back.

So on this morning, in what he calculated was the last month of his career in the stock market—a career that had taken the family estate in Plaquemens County into its third mortgage, the property having been free and clear since 1732 under a grant from the House of Bourbon— Ferdinand De Chef Hunt chose to pop papers up in high arcs behind his back into little wastebaskets.

He was twenty-eight years old, darkly handsome, and with the million-dollar inheritance left him by his mother four years ago, a self-made broke.

"Better not do that," said a customers' man behind him. "Dalton and Harrow themselves are here."

"In New Orleans?"

"Yeah, they got here real early. Locked themselves in the boss's private office, sent out for a personnel file, saw the boss for a couple of hours, then nothing."

"They're closing down the New Orleans operation," Hunt said.

"They can't. We're one of their more successful offices."

"Which means we're going broke slower than the others. Watch, you'll see. We're going under. I'm only sorry it didn't happen a few years ago when I still had money for lunch."

"If you think I'm flipping cards with you again for lunch, fella, you're off your num-num."

"Mumbletypeg?"

"I saw you in the park with that penknife. It looked like it had strings on it."

"Darts?"

"You were drunk for a week on darts. You were the only guy on Bourbon Street with cash in his pocket."

"Pool? Golf? Tennis? Squash? Skittleball?"

"Today I eat lunch. Hunt, if I had your talent, I'd turn

pro. I'd be out on the golf circuit tomorrow. The tennis circuit. I'd hustle pool."

"Can't. I promised Mother. I can't use it for money."

"You call your talent 'it.' I never understood that."

"Good," said Hunt and was glad the conversation was interrupted by a secretary who said he was wanted in the manager's office.

"Should I clean out my desk now or after?" asked Hunt.

"I don't think ever," said the secretary, and she brought him to the main office where he recognized two men because he had seen their portraits on the office walls. Winthrop Dalton and V. Rodefer Harrow III. They both wore dark striped suits with vests. Dalton had the gaunt gray-haired probity of old New York State wealth. Harrow was fatter, with delicate jowls and weak blue eyes. He was as bald as a bicuspid.

"You're the De Chef lad, aren't you?" asked Dalton. He sat on the right of the office manager's desk, Harrow on the left. The office manager was out.

"Well, sir, yes, you might say so. Except that on my father's side I'm a Hunt. L. Hunt of Texarkana. Maybe you've heard of him. Electrical contracting. Soroptimist's man of the year, 1954. First exalted ruler of the Arkansas Elks. Largest distributor in the South for the Vermillion Socket."

"Can't say that I have," said Dalton. "Sit down and tell us about your mother. Specifically, her father."

"Well, he's dead, sir."

"Sorry to hear that. Did he have any other offspring?"

"Yes, he had a son."

Hunt saw V. Rodefer Harrow's jowls quiver.

"And where does your uncle live?" asked Dalton.

"He died as a child. He was three. A hunting accident. It sounds crazy explaining it," said Hunt, sitting tentatively in one of the fine leather chairs purchased by the office in

81

better days. He sat with his hands on the polished wooden arm rests as if ready to leave instantly on command.

"Tell us about it. We know the world is made of many strange things. The perfect truth itself is strange."

"Well, he was drowned in a feeder stream."

"Nothing strange about that," said Dalton.

"It was what he was doing at the time, sir. He was hunting, if you can believe it."

"I do. And at what age did you start hunting?"

"Well, grandpa—my mother's father—started me young, and then he died, and Ma made me promise never to do it again, and I just haven't hunted since. And when she died, she left me the place up at Plaquemens, his place. Uh, he died of a heart attack. And, well, with the estate, the first mortgage on it, I went into business. I joined Dalton, Harrow, Petersen and Smith. And I don't hunt."

"You said 'it.' What's 'it'?"

"Oh, like a talent we have. I'd rather not discuss the subject."

"I'd rather you would."

"Well, sir, it's personal."

"I can see your reluctance. Both V. Rodefer and I can understand your reluctance. But we'd like you to trust us. As friends."

"As friends," said V. Rodefer Harrow III.

"As good friends," said Winthrop Dalton.

"I'd rather not, sir, it's really embarrassing."

"Friends shouldn't be embarrassed in front of friends," said Winthrop Dalton. "Are you embarrassed in front of me, V. Rodefer?"

"I'm too rich to be embarrassed," said V. Rodefer Harrow III.

"My apologies for V. Rodefer. He's from the coast. Please continue."

"Well, we have a special talent in our family. At least

on my mother's side. It has to do with objects. It sounds simple, but it's really complicated, and its got a sordid history, and my mother made me promise never to pass it on. And it looks like I'm not going to because I don't have a son."

"We know that, but wouldn't you teach it to someone else?" asked Dalton.

"It's not something you can exactly teach. You can only teach it to certain persons, you know. Some people can tell where an object is by feel, and there's a certain hereditary thing at work here also, if you know what I mean."

"You've got the 'it' then?"

"Oh, yeah. Just as if my father's side had been De Chef."

Harrow's jowls jiggled in delight.

"Could you show it to us, the it, of course?" said Winthrop Dalton.

"Sure," said Hunt rising from the chair. He collected a piece of note paper, a pen, a calendar, popped them once lightly in an upturned palm and, then, announcing "the wastebasket there," flipped the pen sideways, then the calendar, and then with a skimming slash of his hand hurled the paper aloft. The pen, like a small spear, hit point first and rattled into the bottom of the metal pail. The calendar clunked in on a direct line, and the paper veered up, then around, settled to the right of the basket, and then leaned left and in.

"With the paper, it's the air. Paper is the most complicated. Like the real secret is your not working with constants. People only know it when they, say, fire a gun and there's a stiff cross breeze. I mean like twenty knots. Know what I mean? Or golfers on a muggy day, it's really got to be muggy though, and then they realize they're not working with a constant. It's really a form of sensitivity, knowing where everything is in relationship to everything

83

else and its mass, of course. Most people consider air nothing, but it isn't. It's a thing. Like water or that desk. Air's a thing."

"This skill you have works with all objects?" asked Winthrop Dalton. V. Rodefer Harrow leaned forward over his paunch, the light shining on his tightly stretched dome.

"Sure."

"Let's go to a golf course," said Dalton. "For a friendly round."

"A thousand dollars a hole," said Harrow.

"I don't have—I hate to say it for a man in the market, but I don't have a thousand dollars."

"That's very typical of men in the market. How much do you have?"

"I have thirty-five, no, thirty-three cents. I bought a Danish. That's what I have."

"We'll play for that," said Harrow.

"I don't have greens fees."

"We'll take care of it. Do you have clubs? Never mind, we'll get you clubs. Don't think of yourself as poor just because you don't have money. We suffer reversals too, but the key to our 'it,' so to speak, is that we don't think of ourselves as poor. And we don't want you to either."

"Absolutely not," said V. Rodefer Harrow.

If it had not been these two particular men, Ferdinand De Chef Hunt would have been embarrassed to be out on the course with two men in vests and rolled up sleeves and street shoes.

Dalton had argued with the club pro over the price of rented clubs, something that would have withered Hunt's pride, if it had not been *the* Winthrop Dalton who had done it. Dalton asked for the cheapest balls.

When Dalton teed off on the par four 425-yard first hole, he sliced viciously into underbrush that lined Lake Ponchartrain. He delayed other starts behind him for twenty minutes while looking for the ball, even though he found two others in the process.

Young Hunt drove a not quite respectable 165 yards, but the drive was ruler-straight down the fairway. The breeze off the lake invigorated him. The grass was freshly cut and smelled good, the sun was warm and Ferdinand De Chef Hunt forgot about the stock market as completely as he could.

His second shot was 150 yards, again straight down the fairway, and V. Rodefer Harrow, riding in the cart, commented that he wasn't seeing anything impressive. Then Hunt hit his six iron a looping long, perfect parabola directly at the pin.

"Whew," whistled Harrow.

"Ah," said Dalton.

"Easy," said Hunt. He tapped in a two-inch putt for a par four.

"We each owe you thirty-three cents," said Dalton. "That's sixty-six cents." He had Harrow count the change out of his pocket.

"Let's play for sixty-six cents each. I want to get my money back," said Dalton. "Don't you, V. Rodefer?"

"Absolutely," said Harrow, who had scored a nine with cheating. Dalton had a seven with a good putt.

The next was another par four, which Hunt made with identical shots, including a four-inch putt after a magnificent six iron.

"Now you've got a dollar thirty-two. Let's go for double or nothing."

"This is a par three, 170 yards. I'm super on those," said Hunt.

"Let's see how super."

Super was a birdie two, and Hunt found himself playing for $2.64 on the next hole. As they went down fairways and on to putting greens, his new friends asked him about the "it," each time doubling the bet and saying they had

85

to have a chance to get back their money. By the seventh hole they were playing for $42.24, and Hunt was positively expansive with his new friends.

His mother, he told them, had made him promise never to use the "it" for a living because of the sordid past of the talent. The talent was not always used in sporting events. Originally it had been used with knives and guns for profit. De Chef was an old French name. It went back to a servant in the court of Louis XIV. The servant was an assistant chef, but to give him the right to kill royalty, the king had to make him royalty. The whole thing came about when an Oriental murderer—there was no other word for it—came to the court at the request of the king. Hunt didn't know how much history Dalton and Harrow knew, but at that time the Sun King, as Louis was called, was having trouble with the lords. He wanted to unify the nation. Well, this murderer took some sort of a dislike to France. He wasn't a Chinaman was the only description that had been passed down in the De Chef family. But he didn't like France. And the king who had a lot of respect—well, it was probably fear—said he would pay a large amount of money to this guy to teach a few of his loyal lords some of what he could do. The Oriental was supposed to be amazing.

"We think you're amazing," said Harrow, counting out $169 in bills and pushing them into Hunt's pocket as they stepped off the tenth green and headed back toward the clubhouse.

"No. This guy was supposed to be. I mean what I'm doing was nothing, or at least not much. In any case, none of the lords could quite pick it up, and this Oriental finds the assistant chef can learn, and the king says a commoner can't kill royalty, so to solve the problem like they always do in France, they found a bastardy thing somewhere whereby my ancestor had noble blood and therefore, picking up the 'it' from the Oriental, he could

86

go out and zonk any nobility the king wished. When the family moved from France, before the revolution, they sort of made their money the same way until my mother. And she said enough is enough and made me promise never to use the talent for money."

"A noble thought and promise," said Dalton. "But if something is wrong and untrue, then it's not noble, is it?"

"Well, I guess not," said Hunt, who, having won $337.92, offered to pay for dinner. And when he did so, when he had paid out nearly $200 for dinner at Maxim's for three and he had already spent part of his winnings, Winthrop Dalton informed him he had already broken his promise to his mother.

"But it only started with thirty-three cents. I always used to play for lunches and things and maybe drinks and a few bucks."

"Well, it's now three hundred and thirty-seven dollars and ninety-two cents."

"I'll give it back."

"That won't unbreak the promise, and frankly we don't want it back. It was a pleasure to see you in action."

"It certainly was," said Harrow. "Probably one of life's fifteen best thrills."

"Does it hurt to have broken that promise?" asked Dalton.

"It does now," said Hunt.

"But it didn't until you told yourself so. When you had broken the promise without knowing it, the whole thing felt fine, yes or no?"

"Well, yes," said Hunt.

"Are you your own friend or your enemy?" said Harrow.

"I guess I'm my friend."

"Then why do you make yourself feel bad?"

"I, uh, made a promise."

"Right. And in your attitude toward that promise you're ready to take food out of your own mouth, force yourself to live in a slum—you're broke—and in general hurt yourself. Do you really think you deserve to hurt yourself?"

"Well, no."

"Then why do you do it?"

"I was taught a promise is a promise."

"You were taught a lot of things, and so was I, a lot of things that made me miserable and unhappy and, frankly, a hateful person," said Dalton.

"You can leave here broke," said Harrow. "You can return the money. You can even owe us for this meal and go without lunches for a month to repay me with money I don't need. Will that make you happy?"

"Of course not," said Hunt.

"Then that's pretty stupid, isn't it?"

"Yes, it is."

Dalton stretched a veined hand out over the youthful shoulder.

"Tell me, son, aren't you a little bit tired of being stupid, of hurting yourself, of making your one life miserable. Aren't you?"

"I guess, yes."

"You guess yes. You don't know?" asked Dalton. "Are you stupid?"

"No."

"Then stop acting like it," said Dalton. "What we're getting at is that you'd be pretty stupid to starve, trying to keep a promise that's already broken."

"I'll keep the money," said Hunt.

"Well, son, there's just a little bit more. We want you to be rich and happy. Will you join us in making you rich and happy?"

"Will you?" asked V. Rodefer Harrow III.

"Yes, sir," said Ferdinand De Chef Hunt.

88

Dalton leaned forward. "We want you to meet the most wonderful person on earth. He's only fifteen years old, and he knows more than all of us put together about how to make people happy. Important people too. You'd be surprised."

"He's right here in America now," said Harrow.

"Praised be his blissful name," said Winthrop Dalton.

"All praise be to his perfect blissfulness," said V. Rodefer Harrow III.

© Lorillard 1975

Come for the filter...

A PRODUCT OF
Lorillard

KENT

WITH
THE FAMOUS MICRONITE FILTER

DELUXE LENGTH

...you'll stay for the taste.

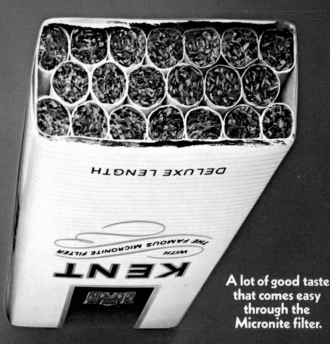

DELUXE LENGTH

KENT

WITH THE FAMOUS MICRONITE FILTER

A lot of good taste that comes easy through the Micronite filter.

18 mg. "tar," 1.2 mg. nicotine av. per cigarette, FTC Report Oct. '74.

CHAPTER EIGHT

Dr. Harold W. Smith looked with pinched eyes at the stapled-together pile of papers on his large plain metal desk.

"Lease Agreement," it was headed, and he read through the whereases, which were contradicted by the "be it noted howevers," and the wherefores, which were watered down by the "except in the event ofs," and automatically translated them into English to learn that the Divine Bliss Mission, Inc., had leased Kezar Stadium in San Francisco for one night, four days hence "for purposes of a religious meeting."

The lease agreement was signed for the Divine Bliss Mission, Inc., by one Gasphali Krishna, also known as Irving Rosenblatt, who bore the title of "Chief Arch-Priest, California district." A stamped notation on the last page of the lease recorded it as "paid in full."

Smith read the lease again. This was it, "the big thing." He had no doubt about it, but what was a big thing about a revival tent meeting, no matter what kind of stadium it was held in? From Billy Sunday through Aimee Semple McPherson through Father Divine and Prophet Jones and

Billy Graham and Oral Roberts, millions of people had been led up to someone else's vision of God for periods of sometimes as long as two days, and the country was none the worse for it. What was this Indian juvenile delinquent going to do that was different?

Of course, there was the list of names that Remo had given Smith of the maharaji's followers. Some of them highly placed and important people. But so what? What were they going to do that could somehow justify all this effort that Smith's organization was putting into a teenage Indian boy?

Smith let his eyes wander off the lease form again. If it had not been for the fact that a number of Americans who had gone to Patna had disappeared, and the Indian government had refused to show any concern about it, Smith realized he would seriously question whether this was any of CURE's business at all. There was just nothing there in all he had seen so far that represented a threat to the government. And that was, after all, CURE's one and only mission—the preservation of constitutional government. It was why CURE had been created by a now dead president and why Smith had been put in charge of it, and it was why only two people besides the president in office—Smith and Remo—knew what CURE was and what it did.

From a standpoint of secrecy, CURE made the Manhattan Project look like a meeting of Greenwich Village Democratic committeemen. And why not? The Manhattan Project had produced only the atomic bomb, but CURE's secrecy might be even more important, for if CURE should be exposed, it would be an admission that constitutional government hadn't worked and didn't work, and it might bring the entire nation down.

Dr. Smith put aside the lease form. He had made up his mind. Remo was working on the case, and he would let that continue before deciding whether or not to assign

Remo to other things. And just as a precaution, he would take Remo's list of names and see that they were immobilized before the Kezar Stadium Blissathon of the Maharaji Dor. Something, perhaps, under the cover of a required hospital examination. And that would cover all the bases for a while. But he wished he had the names of all Dor's American followers. Remo had said there were more.

Smith looked at the computer terminal recessed under a glass panel on his desk, which silently and continuously printed summary conclusions of the data gathered by thousands of agents across the country, agents who thought they were working for the FBI and the tax bureau and as customs inspectors and bank examiners, but all of whose reports wound up in CURE's computers.

A sign here, a loose word there, a change in prices somewhere else, and the computer could draw conclusions and put them on Smith's desk, along with recommended actions.

The computer silently printed:

"Possible foreign money influx, unsettling prices on Midwest grain exchange. No recommendation."

It paused. Then:

"Aircraft company near bankruptcy now appears solvent again. Investigate potential ties with Arab oil countries."

Such reports moved across his desk all day long. They were the day-to-day essence of his job, Smith reminded himself. The important things. Things that could affect America's security, its position in the world.

Maybe he had been wrong. Maybe Remo should get off this Divine Bliss Mission business right away. He may have overreacted in assigning him in the first place.

Smith looked down at the computer, again silently forming letters under the glass panel.

"Policeman's slaying in Midwest apparently linked to

93

battle for control of crime syndicate in that part of country. Crime figures have close connections with several United States senators, and certain immigration bills affecting those crime figures have been introduced by those senators."

Now that was important, Smith thought. Crime had even reached its tentacles into the U.S. Senate. That was a case perhaps for Remo's talents.

The computer kept forming letters.

"Suggest pressure upon senators, to get them to lift political protection from mob figures."

Probably the right approach, Smith thought. And probably the next assignment for Remo.

The computer kept printing.

"All praise the Divine Blissful Master. Bliss be his."

And Smith shuddered.

And 2700 miles away, across the nation, Martin Mandelbaum was also shuddering, with outrage.

He would read them the goddam riot act. That was for sure. He would ream them up and he would ream them down. How could they? For Christ's sake, how could they?

As he walked along the polished marble floors of San Francisco's central airport terminal, he got angrier and angrier.

Who was that fat-faced little punk?

Along every wall, on every column, on every litter basket, everywhere in his nice clean terminal was a poster of this fat-faced, fruity-looking boy with a half-assed fuzz of a mustache. Who the hell was he?

Under the color picture were a few lines of type. They read:

HE IS COMING.
TUESDAY NIGHT.

KEZAR STADIUM.
ALL ARE INVITED.
ADMISSION FREE.

Who the hell was HE?

And how the hell did all these goddam posters get into Martin Mandelbaum's beautiful, clean airport?

HE, whoever HE was, had some fine frigging nerve, and the maintenance men who worked under Mandelbaum's direction were going to hear about it.

Mandelbaum angrily yanked down one sign from a stone pillar and marched into the corridor that led to his office.

"Good morning, Mr. Mandelbaum," said his secretary.

"Get everybody," he growled. "Everybody. Broom pushers, toilet scrubbers, wall cleaners, painters, plumbers, everybody. Get 'em in the meeting room in five minutes."

"Everybody?"

"Yes, Miss Perkins, fucking everybody."

Mandelbaum went into his office, slamming the door behind him. He would ream ass. As he had in World War II as a top sergeant, as he had on his way when he got his first civilian job that put him in charge of two other people, as he had while he worked his way up the bureaucratic ladder, as he had all his life.

It was just not possible that vandals had sneaked into the airport during the night and plastered it with posters of HE. Mandelbaum looked at the poster in his hand.

What a stupid-looking creep. Why the hell hadn't his maintenance men seen them defacing the airport?

"HE," Mandelbaum said out loud to the poster, "keep outa my frigging airport."

He hacked in the back of his throat and put a glemmy squarely between the eyes of Maharaji Gupta Mahesh Dor, the Blissful Master, then threw the poster in the waste-paper basket beside his desk, and began pacing up and

95

down, counting to himself the five minutes he had to wait.

It was worth the wait. It was beautiful. He reamed up and he reamed down. One hundred and forty men sat there in stolid, embarrassed silence as Martin Mandelbaum told them what he thought of their efforts to keep the airport terminal clean, along with a few suggestions concerning the morality of their mothers and the lack of virility of their reputed fathers.

"Now get out of here," he finally said. "Get out of here and get down every picture of that fat-faced fucking frog, and if you see anybody else putting up any more of them, call the cops and have the bastards arrested. And if you want to beat the shit out of them first, that's all right too. Now get out of here." He looked around and saw his second-in-command, a red-faced, retired Irish cop named Kelly, sitting quietly in a front row seat. "Kelly, you make sure the goddam job is done right."

Kelly nodded, and since Mandelbaum's speech was not exactly calculated to inspire open discussion, the 140 workers silently got to their feet and headed out the door of the big auditorium-style meeting room. In masses they swept through the main terminal building ripping down the pictures of Maharaji Dor.

"What'll we do with these?" one man asked.

"I'll take them," Kelly said. "I'll get rid of them. Don't rip them. Maybe I can sell them for junk." He chuckled and began to collect the posters, piled up into his outstretched arms.

"I'll get rid of them, boys," he told the workers who were going through the building like a swarm of ants devouring a scrap of meat. "Don't leave even a single one. We don't want the Jew on our backs again, do we?" And he winked.

And the workers winked back despite the fact that they knew a man who called Mandelbaum "the Jew" behind

96

his back would have no compunctions about calling them "the nigger" or "the spick" or "the wop" behind their backs.

His arms were full, but the terminal was whiskbroom clean when Kelly, sweating under his load of cardboard posters, walked from the main terminal area toward the back of the building where the workers' lockers were.

He set the pile of pictures on a wooden table in the deserted locker room, and with a key opened a tall gray standup locker in the corner.

The door opened. Taped to the inside of it was a poster of Maharaji Gupta Mahesh Dor.

Kelly looked around to see that there was no one else in the locker room, then leaned forward and kissed the picture on the befuzzed lips.

"Don't worry, Blissful Master," he said softly, "the Jew will not prevail against your wonder."

He put the piles of posters into the back of the locker very carefully. After Mandelbaum went home, he would return for them and put them back up.

Just as he had last night.

CHAPTER NINE

"You surprised me, kid. You didn't look like the patriotic-American type," said Remo.

Joleen Snowy ignored him. She remained kneeling on the ground at the foot of the steps leading from the Air India jet, kissing the blacktop surface, her arms extended full in front of her as in supplication, her butt raised winsomely toward the plane.

"Oh, wondrous America," she moaned. "Land of all beauty and bliss."

Remo looked at Chiun, who stood beside him.

"Oh, marvelousness of the West. Oh, repository of that which is good."

"See," said Remo. "A patriot."

"Beauteous beneficence. Vessel of purity," Joleen wailed.

"I think she overdoes it," said Chiun. "What about racism? What about Gatewater?"

"Just details," Remo said. He grabbed Joleen by her right elbow. "Okay, kid, up and at 'em."

She stood up straight, very close to Remo, smiling into his face, and under the silver stripe down her forehead and the darkening eye makeup, the face of a very young woman could still be seen. "I just want to thank you for bringing me to this great land."

"Well, shucks," said Remo modestly. "It's good, all right, but it's got its faults. Even I've got to admit that."

"It has no faults," said Joleen petulantly. "It is all perfect."

"Why did you leave then?" asked Remo, steering the girl toward the terminal.

"I left because the Blissful Master was in India and it was perfect. And now that the Blissful Master is in America . . ."

"Right," Remo concluded with disgust, "America is perfect now." She had been loose when he found her, she had been loose on the plane, and she was still as loose as a pail of killies.

He turned toward Chiun and shrugged. Chiun confided to him: "Anyone who would allow an Ilhibad tribesman out of the hills to defend himself is capable of anything. If the girl is a follower of his, she is defective in the head. She must be watched."

They moved through the doors into the main terminal, and as they stepped inside, Joleen let out a wail and pulled away from Remo. Inside the terminal, people turned to see where the scream had come from. They saw a girl in a pink wrap bolt forward into the terminal building, running at top speed, stopping only at a stone column, which she embraced with both arms, and began to deposit kisses upon.

"Now this is getting silly, Chiun," said Remo.

"It is your problem. I wish only to get on the vessel to return to Sinanju, and not be deprived of it by your tricks."

"You're the one who decided not to go," Remo said, watching the back of Joleen, who was still kissing the column.

100

"Only because there was an obligation to meet, now it is met and I wish to go home. If this were a dec country with people who kept their promises, I would no have to feel this way, but as it is . . ."

"Right, right, right, right," said Remo.

He walked away to collect Joleen Snowy. She had left the first column and was now embracing a second one. Remo saw what she had been slopping kisses onto. There was a poster on the column showing Maharaji Gupta Mahesh Dor. Remo shook his head. He looked like a brown toad. A brown toad with a mustache that wasn't ever going to make it.

As he drew close to Joleen, he heard her babbling, "O Divine Blissfulness. O Most Perfect Master." Every word was punctuated with the smack of wet kisses. "Your servant awaits you again, with open body, the vessel upon which you may work your perfect will."

"Don't talk dirty," said Remo, lifting her by the waist and pulling her from the pillar.

"Do not make into dirt something that is pure and beautiful and religious. I am his handmaiden."

"He looks like he could be a dirty old man," said Remo, "except he really lacks the character. He looks more like a dirty young boy with fuzz on his lip."

Chiun joined them, and Remo steered Joleen Snowy toward the front door of the terminal. "He is the perfect master," she screeched. "All blissfulness. All peace and love come to those who truly love him. I have been among the chosen."

She continued her caterwauling into a taxicab, while Remo was trying to tell the driver their destination.

"He is bliss. He is beauty. He is power."

"She is nuts," Remo told the driver. "Take us into the city. I'll tell you where when she runs down."

But Joleen would not stop.

"All bliss. All perfection. All peace. All love," she shrieked.

"Cabbie, pull over here," said Remo. When the cab driver pulled to the curb, Remo leaned toward the front seat so the driver could hear him.

"Is this noise driving you nuts?" Remo asked.

The cabbie nodded. "I thought she was like your kid sister or something," he shouted.

Remo shook his head and reached into his pocket. He handed forward a fifty dollar bill. "Look. This is a tip in advance. Now how about going into that diner down the block and getting a cup of coffee? Give me five minutes."

The cabbie half turned in his seat and looked at Remo carefully. "You're not thinking of any funny stuff, are you? Just last week, some guys attacked a driver's meter."

"I never attacked a meter in my life," said Remo. "Come on now. Five minutes."

"Do I keep the key?"

Remo nodded.

The cabbie looked at the fifty dollar bill in Remo's hand, shrugged, plucked it from Remo's fingers, and stuffed it into the pocket of his yellow plaid shirt. "Time for my break anyway."

He pushed open the door and walked away from the cab, pocketing the key.

"All truth. All beauty. All wonder. All marvelousness."

"Chiun, would you go for a walk?" asked Remo.

"I will not. I will not be driven from this cab by the wailing of any banshee. Besides, this neighborhood does not look safe."

"All right, Little Father, but don't say I didn't warn you."

Remo turned to Joleen Snowy, still shrieking, and put a

hand under her left breast, finding a nerve just between the flesh and the rib cage, and gave it a twitch.

"Oh, sensitivity, oh perfect, oh, oh, oh, oh, oh," she said.

"Oh, disgusting," Chiun said. "You Americans are like horses in a pasture." His hands seemed not to move, but then he was out of the cab, and the door slammed behind him with a thunk that would do nothing for the door lock's longevity.

Alone in the cab with Joleen, Remo said: "You want bliss? I'll give you bliss."

And he did.

At one end of the street the cabdriver sipped coffee.

At the other end, Chiun found a store window filled with tape recorders and transistor radios and portable television sets, all of which looked interesting and worth possessing, until he saw they had been made in Japan.

He forced himself to stay there for exactly 300 seconds, then went back to the cab. He got in the back door and sat next to Remo and Joleen Snowy. He said nothing.

A few minutes later the cabdriver returned. He glanced with suspicion into the quiet back seat to make sure that Remo had not murdered the screecher.

Joleen sat quietly between Remo and Chiun. Her only sound was an occasional moan. "Mmmmmmmmmm." She smiled a lot.

The cabdriver drove off.

"Mmmmmm. Bliss. Peace. Mmmmmmmmm." Joleen Snowy put her arms about Remo's neck. "You are a perfect master too."

Chiun snickered. Remo looked out the window in disgust.

Ten minutes later, Remo was in a telephone booth. Across Market Street in San Francisco, a digital clock outside a bank building flashed the hour, minute, and second: 11:59:17.

Remo was not comfortable with that time; it seemed to him that it was later. He wore no watch, he had not for years, but he did not believe 11:59: now 22.

Remo dialed the phone, calling a toll-free 800 area code number. On the first ring, Smith answered.

"Just in time," he said. "I was about to cut this line for the day."

"What time is it?" asked Remo.

"Twelve-oh-two and fifteen seconds," he answered.

"I knew it," said Remo. "The clock here is wrong."

"So of what importance is that? Most clocks are wrong."

"Yeah," said Remo. "I knew it was wrong, but I didn't know how much. I haven't been that much off time in years."

"Maybe it's jet lag," said Smith.

"I don't have any jet lag, whatever that is," said Remo.

"Forget it. Any report?"

"We've been to Patna, but the little toad skipped before we got there."

"Where are you now?"

"San Francisco. His most Blissful Bullshit is having some kind of rally here in a couple of days."

"Yes," said Smith. "I presume that's the 'big thing' we've been hearing about."

"Guess so. He's been collecting Baptist ministers."

"Baptist ministers? What for?"

"I don't know. Maybe converts or something. When I find him, I'll find out. Chiun is on my back. He wants to go to Sinanju right away."

"Remo, it'll have to wait. CURE's been compromised. Someplace in here we've got one of the maharaji's people."

"Why not? He's got them everywhere. Did you drop all

104

those people off the Empire State Building like I told you to?"

"No. But they're all going into hospitals for medical examinations until after the maharaji leaves the country. You said there were other names, other followers, that the man in San Diego didn't know."

"Yeah."

"See if you can find out who they are. It's just a feeling I have, but maybe this 'big thing' had something to do with his American followers."

"Could be."

"Do you need any help?" asked Smith.

"Well, a brass band might be good to let everybody know that Chiun and I are here. A couple of flamethrower units and a division of artillery, and I think we should be able to handle his eminent fatness. Of course, we don't need any help. Nothing your computers can give us anyway. What time is it?"

"Twelve-five and ten seconds."

"Dammit, I'm off. See you, Smitty. Stay within your budget."

Inside the cab, as Remo walked back toward it, Joleen asked Chiun: "Are you his friend?"

"I am no one's friend but my own."

"Well, you seem so close."

"He is my pupil. He is backward, but we do the best we can, considering. He is more a son than a friend."

"I don't understand."

"If you no longer like a friend, you end friendship. With sons it is different. If you no longer like them, they are still your sons."

"That's right, buddy," said the cabdriver. "I got one like that. Big lug. All-state football in high school and the team. So I work to put him through school. So he gets a scholarship to USC for it. But he was too lazy to make out of school, and do you think he'll look for work?

105

Not on your life. He says he's waiting for a position. He can't take just any job."

"I am not interested in the activities of your cretinous offspring," said Chiun.

"Yeah, a position," the cabdriver said, not having heard one word of Chiun's. "Did you ever hear of anything like that? He can't take a job; he has to have a position?"

"I have a position for you," said Chiun. "Prone. Mouth stuffed into dirt. Silent."

Remo slid back into the cab.

"Well?" said Chiun.

"Well, what?"

"When does our vessel leave?"

"Not for a while, I'm afraid," said Remo. He gave the cabdriver an address on Union Street.

Chiun folded his arms across his chest. Joleen watched him, then looked at Remo, who said, "It can't be helped. It's business, Little Father. That comes first."

She turned toward Chiun. "It should not come before promises," said Chiun.

"We've got this little thing to do first," said Remo.

Joleen pingponged her head between them.

"But what is a promise made by a white man?" Chiun asked himself. "A nothing," he answered himself. "A nothing made by a nothing, signifying nothing and worth nothing. Remo, you are a nothing. Smith is a nothing."

"Right, Little Father," Remo said. "And don't forget racists."

"And you are both racists. I have never heard of anything like this. A broken promise. The ingratitude. You would not do this to one whose skin was as fish-flesh pale as your own."

"Right," said Remo. "We're racists through and through, Smitty and me."

"That is correct."

"And our word can't be trusted."

106

"That is also correct."

Remo turned to Joleen. "Do you know he taught me everything I know?"

Joleen nodded. "Yes, he told me."

"He would have."

"He is right, you know," said Joleen.

"About what?"

"You are a racist."

"Who says?" asked Remo.

"Everyone knows. All Americans are racists."

"Right, child," said Chiun. "It is the defense adopted by the inferior person."

CHAPTER TEN

In an alley off Union Street in San Francisco, hippie hucksters hawk homemades. Jewelry, painted shells and stones, leather belts fill up little stalls that line both sides of the alley.

Business is generally bad, but the salesmen do not seem to mind, content instead to sit in the sun, smoking marijuana, and talking among themselves about how nice it will be when the revolution comes and the new socialist government will pay them for sitting there.

In the rear, the alley opened into a gravel-coated yard, fenced in with high wooden stockade posts. Booths bordered the entire yard, and one of the booths flaunted the poster of the Maharji Gupta Mahesh Dor.

Joleen dropped to her knees and kissed the steel cable that the poster was taped to.

"O Blissful Master," she said. "Across the seas, I come following your goodness."

"Don't pull on the frigging wire," said a bearded, tanned blond youth, shirtless, with rag-cuff jeans, a silver earring, and a grape juice concession.

From the booths along the fence, people turned, mostly young women, looking at Joleen.

"They smell bad," Chiun told Remo.

Remo shrugged.

"Are these flower people?" asked Chiun.

Remo nodded.

"Why do they not smell like flowers?"

"Smelling good is part of the capitalist conspiracy," said Remo.

Chiun sniffed. "It doesn't matter. All whites smell funny anyway."

The blond man with the beard was now yanking Joleen to her feet. She struggled to stay in her kneeling position, her hands tightly clenching the wire that anchored the pole holding up the small hinged roof of the grape juice shed.

"I said, get the frig out of there," the youth said.

Remo moved toward Joleen, but a voice echoed through the yard.

"Cease!"

It came from the end of the yard. Faces turned toward the voice.

A man stood there. He had come from a door in the fence, between two booths. He wore a pink robe that came down to the top of silver-sandaled feet. Down his forehead was painted a silver stripe that matched Joleen's.

"Let her be," he intoned. "She is of the faith."

'She's got no goddam business hanging onto my roof wire," the blond youth said. He tugged again at Joleen's kneeling body.

The man in the robe clapped his hands together, twice, sharply.

The young women in the booths turned, as if on command, and began to advance slowly toward Joleen and the blond man. The youth kept tugging at Joleen, then looked up. He saw a dozen young women moving toward him, their faces expressionless, their feet, mostly sandal-clad, scuffing rhythmically in the gravel, like the sound of a railroad locomotive slowly pulling away from a station.

"Hey," he said. "Okay. Just kidding, you know. I just didn't want her to . . ."

They were on him then. Four women in front bore him to the ground with their weight. They sprawled their bodies upon him, pinning him, and then the others moved forward and began to strike at him, at his face and body, with hands and feet.

Joleen hung grimly to the steel wire, murmuring, "Blissful One, oh, most Blissful One."

The man at the end of the yard looked toward Remo and Chiun and smiled at them, a smile that showed neither warmth nor embarrassment, then clapped his hands twice again.

At the sharp sound, the dozen women who had fallen upon the blond man stopped, rose to their feet, and shuffled back toward their booths.

"You will be gone in an hour," the man intoned toward the youth who lay bruised and bloody on the gravel of the yard. "You are not worthy of lodging here."

The man lowered his voice and directed his words toward Joleen. "Come, child of Patna, bliss awaits you."

As if on command, Joleen rose and walked toward the end of the yard. Remo and Chiun followed.

"And have you business with us?" the man asked Remo.

"We brought her from India," Remo said. "From Patna." On a hunch, he flashed the gold shield he had picked up in Patna on the floor of Dor's Palace.

"Actually," Chiun said, "we were on our way to Sinanju, but we were stopped by a white man's promise."

"Oh, yes, Sinanju," the man said, a note of confusion in his voice. "Come in." He nodded knowingly to Remo.

111

He led them through the door in the fence and through a garden with large, smelly, tropical-appearing flowers, then into the back door of a building and into a large sun-lit room that had been carved from four smaller rooms on the first floor of an old home that fronted on another street.

The room was immaculately clean. In it were nine young women, wearing long white gowns that flounced out around them as they sat on the floor, sewing.

They looked up at the four people entering the room.

"Children of bliss," the man in the pink robe said, clapping his hands to bring them to attention. "These voyagers are from Patna."

The young women, whose faces were white, whose hair was yellow and brown and black, rose to their feet and suddenly were clustered around Joleen.

"Have you seen him?"

Joleen nodded.

"And shared in his perfection?"

Joleen nodded.

"Make her at home among you," the man said, and motioned Remo and Chiun to follow him toward a side room.

Behind them was the happy chatter of the young women.

"What of the Master?" one said.

"He is perfect," said Joleen.

Chiun paused and nodded.

"And what of his perfection?" another asked.

"He is of perfect perfection."

Chiun nodded again, more vigorously this time.

Joleen warmed to her work. "He is the wisdom of all wisdom, the Master, the goodness of all that is good."

Chiun agreed with that.

Remo leaned to him. "Chiun, they're talking about the maharaji."

"No," said Chiun, disbelievingly.

"Yes," said Remo.

"Americans are all fools."

As Remo followed the priest and Chiun into the office, he turned. The nine girls had swelled in number to some fifteen. One whispered in Joleen's ear, and Joleen blushed and nodded. The girl clapped. "You must tell us all."

"I wanted to go to Holy Patna too," another girl complained. "But my father took away my Diner's Club Card."

"Come," one girl called to the newer arrivals into the house. "Meet Sister Joleen. She has been to Patna and seen the Master. She has . . ."

Remo closed the door behind him. The man in the pink robe was sliding behind the desk and graciously waving Chiun and Remo into two soft leather chairs facing it.

"Welcome to our house," he said. "I am Gasphali Krishna, chief arch-priest of the California district."

"Where is the Master?" Remo asked.

Krishna shrugged. "All is in readiness for him here. A suite of rooms has been arranged. Even the electronic games for his amusement."

"Yeah, but where is he?" said Remo.

"We have not talked at all," said Krishna. "Are you disciples?"

Chiun said, "He is a disciple. I am I."

"And who is 'I'?"

"I is a person cheated with promises broken by unfeeling racists."

"Chiun, will you please?"

"It is true. It is true. Tell him the story, and ask him if it is not true."

"What is true is that we are here to make sure all is well for the Master's big thing," Remo told Krishna. "For that, we came from Patna."

Chiun laughed softly. "Master," he said derisively.

"We were told to prepare for his coming," said Krishna. "But he may be staying elsewhere."

"In a zoo. With the other frogs," Chiun mumbled.

"Chiun, would you go outside and talk to the girls? Tell them how wonderful the Master is," said Remo.

And thus it was that the Master of Sinanju did go out of the office where Remo and a fake Indian were talking nonsense, and he did talk to the young women gathered about there, and he did tell them the absolute truth, as long as one did not get too specific about whom he was talking about.

"What think you of the Master?"

"He is the noblest, warmest, kindest person on earth," said the Master of Sinanju.

"Is he perfection itself?"

"Some men approach perfection; he has reached it and gone beyond."

"What is the lesson of his way?"

"Do well and love justice and practice mercy and all will be well with you," said the Master of Sinanju.

"How may we approach perfection?"

"By listening to his words and acting on his dictates," said the Master of Sinanju. "That is a jewel of truth I give you."

"Come. Come hear the wise man. Come learn of the wisdom of the East that recognized the bliss and perfection of the Master."

Thus did the Master of Sinanju comport himself, while nearby, in the small office behind the closed door, Remo and Krishna continued to talk.

After the door had closed behind Chiun, Krishna had removed the pink turban from his head with a hoisting movement of both hands and a mass of reddish blond frizzy curls had exploded around his head.

"Man, that's a drag," he said.

"It's tough being in charge," said Remo.

114

"Nah, I'm not in charge of anything. They just give me a title and 20 percent of anything I bring in. Man, I'm like a salesman for bliss. Hey, where's that accent from?"

"Newark, New Jersey," said Remo, annoyed at himself because he was no longer supposed to have an accent.

"Put 'er there, old buddy," said Krishna. "Hoboken myself. Newark's changed."

"So has Hoboken," said Remo as Krishna grabbed his hand and pumped it up and down.

"How'd you get into this business?" asked Krishna.

"Just kind of drifted in," said Remo. "You?"

"Well, revolution, man, was out, like they was starting to shoot back. And I didn't really have much stomach for that Third World bullshit. I mean, I guess you could do something with it if you wanted, but so many bad elements. And then this came along a couple of years ago, so I signed up. Dor wasn't so big then, and they needed professional organizers. So old Irving Rosenblatt was Johnny-on-the-spot. But it's like everything else. They start growing, and they're putting their buttered buns in the best jobs. Hey, you like a drink?"

Remo shook his head.

"Grass or something? I got some great shit in from Hawaii."

"No," said Remo. "I'm tapering off."

"Well, the only thing I hate worse than drinking alone is not drinking."

He went to a small cabinet, pulled a bottle from behind a string of books, and poured himself a full glass of Scotch. Chivas Regal. He smiled at Remo. "When the peasants pay, ride first class."

"Everything ready for the big thing?" asked Remo.

"Damned if I know. That's why I'm graumed. They make me the boss out here, and I'm in for 20 percent, and I'm not complaining, 'cause it's been pretty good. But now, when we got the big Blissathon coming up, do they let me run it? No, they send in all these hotshots from every place else, and I don't even get a look." He angrily gulped at the Scotch. "I know what's going to happen. They're going to tell me that the revenue from the Blissathon, man, well that's not part of the San Francisco receipts, and they're gonna try to beat me out of my 20 percent."

"That's a damn shame," Remo said. "You mean you haven't even been in the planning?"

"Not even a smell. Tell me. What's going to happen? I keep hearing these rumbles about something big."

Remo shrugged and tried, without too much difficulty, to look unhappy. "Orders, pal. You know how it is."

"Yeah, I guess so," said Krishna, sipping heavily again. "Don't worry though. The San Francisco mission will be there in all its glory to cheer on old Blissful."

"You still think the swami's going to show up here?" asked Remo.

"The swami," Krishna laughed. "That's a good one. I don't know. But we've rolled in his ping-pong machine in case he does."

"I want to congratulate you, by the way," Remo said. "You run a pretty tight security ship. That was good with the girls out in the yard. With that blond guy."

"Yeah. Well, the chicks are always your best freedom fighters. It must be a bitch being a woman."

"Oh?"

"Yeah. Otherwise, why are they always running around after bullshit? Like looking for some secret thing or some special way that's going to make everything perfect. What a way to have to live."

Remo nodded. "I see the silver stripe. You've been to Patna, but you seem to have kept your wits about you."

Krishna finished the glass and poured himself another. "Well, you know what they say, you can't crap a crapper. Dor's running the oldest hustle in the books. A little drugs,

116

a lot of sex, and a lot more of make everybody feel good. Wanna blow up your mother? Go ahead. It is the way to bliss. Want to rob your boss or cheat the stockholders? You must if you are to attain bliss."

"And you?"

"When I went to Patna, I had a pretty good idea of what to expect. And it didn't work. I've been on drugs, I've had enough sex, and he couldn't impress me with that. And feeling good? Man, I always feel good. Anyway, I faked it and acted like everybody else, and here I am, a chief arch-priest. And I think they're gonna try to beat me out of my 20 percent. They better not try. If they do, man, I'm going into transcendental meditation."

Remo stood up. "For what it's worth," he said, "I'll give you a good report on the security here. You've got a good operation."

"Thanks. You fellas have a place to stay?"

Remo shook his head.

"Well, stay here. We've got plenty of rooms upstairs. This place used to be a whorehouse."

"I think we'll do that," Remo said. "That way we'll be close to everything. Particularly if Blissful shows up. Tell me something. How do you get your skin that color?"

"Tanning lotion," said Krishna, who had put down his glass and was now trying to stuff his hair back under his pink turban. "You know, that chemical crap. Use a lot of it, it's perfect Indian color. Only thing is when I go to Malibu for the weekends, man, I look like I got yellow jaundice."

The telphone rang. Krishna cleared his throat, and then, in a mock Indian accent, said, "Divine Bliss Mission, may Krishna bring you happiness?"

He listened, then whistled. "No shit," he said. "Thanks for calling."

He hung up the telephone and smiled at Remo. "Christ, I'm glad you're here."

117

"Why?" said Remo.

"We heard a rumble last week that there had been some kind of trouble at the San Diego mission. But everybody was clammed on it. But I just heard. The arch-priest down there, Freddy, done bought the farm. Somebody crushed his neck."

"Who did it?" asked Remo casually.

"They're not sure yet. Everybody in the place split so they wouldn't have to deal with the fuzz."

"You think it might be an attempt on the maharaji?"

Krishna shrugged. "Who knows? But I'll tell you, I'm glad you're here. I don't need any crazy people going around killing up my folks."

"Don't worry," Remo said. "We'll protect you."

CHAPTER ELEVEN

"What is he, Elton?"

"He's an Indian."

"G'wan, Elton, they ain't no more Indians in this country."

"Not that kind of Indian. He's a from India kind of Indian." Elton Snowy leaned across the cigarette-scarred wooden counter and whispered into the florid ear of the bartender: "Like a nigger, he is."

"Sheeit. With your Joleen?" The cooked crab face of the fat man registered disbelief.

Snowy nodded glumly. "Drugs. He must have her on drugs. And I went and sent the nigger preacher to go and get her, and he never came back. He must be on those drugs too."

"Elton, I think things started to go bad when that peckerhead asked for that cup of coffee."

Snowy nodded his head, slowly, thoughtfully. He looked down at the glass of sarsaparilla in his hand.

"We shoulda shot him then," said the bartender. "Yep," he agreed with himself. "We shoulda shot him then."

Snowy, exhausted after a day of rounding up volunteer

warriors for the posse to rescue his daughter, said sharply, "But how would that do anything to this little bastard from India?"

"Show him a lesson. Trouble was we let everybody get uppity. First it was niggers, and then it was Putto Rickens, and then it was real Indians, and now it's these funny Indians who are really niggers. Everybody's stepping all over us. Next thing you know, Catholics are gonna start getting uppity around here."

"Pray God it never comes to that," said Snowy.

"We'd better. 'Cause if they come, the Jews will be right behind them."

The horror of that thought stimulated Snowy's thirst, and he drained his glass of sarsaparilla and put it on the bar with a clunk.

"Want more, Elton?"

"No. That's enough. Well?"

"Whatever you want, I'm with you."

"Good," said Snowy. "Pack yourself a bag. We're leaving tonight."

"We?"

"You and me and Fester and Puling."

"Eeeeyow," said the bartender. "All of us going to San Francisco?"

"Yup."

"Won't that be one hell of a nut-busting time? No wives, neither. Yahoo." His voice was so loud that others further down the bar looked at him, and he moved closer to Snowy and said, "I can't wait, Elton."

"My house tonight. At six."

CHAPTER TWELVE

Out of Frisco, toward the west, toward Japan, which called itself the land of the rising sun but was really the land of the setting sun from America's viewpoint, which might have provided a clue about the ending of World War II, over the Golden Gate Bridge, awkwardly red in the daylight sun, the late morning heat having burned off the fog shroud, the ubiquitous workmen giving the bridge its daily dose of ugly red paint, out off the bridge, onto a highway, then into a tunnel, its open mouth painted with arcs of rainbow color, then back out onto the highway.

He drove with an easy discipline, his mind not on the car or the wheel, his finely tuned body and instincts reacting automatically to the swerve of the road, weighing the mass of the car against the centrifugal force, balanced by the coefficient of friction for the tires, all without thought, just through fingertips and palms connected to arms, connected to spinal cord and brain.

Ferdinand De Chef Hunt had never been on this side of San Francisco before. He had visited the city years earlier on business but had no ambition to see the surrounding countryside.

Hunt had learned early of his ability to manipulate objects, and he regarded places as just more objects, only bigger. He was not curious about places he had not seen.

Another tunnel up ahead. On the rock face above it, white paint had been splashed, like a gigantic Tom Sawyeresque attempt to whitewash not just a fence, but the world. Hunt's sharp eyes picked out an outline under the paint. He slowed the car. Yes, it was the outline of a woman, a forty-foot-high painting of a naked woman, and already the white paint was wearing off, and the woman's voluptuous outlines showed through the paint, and the woman was sexy.

Hunt gave the white paint two more weeks before the elements made it almost perfectly transparent, and he hoped he would still be in the area because he wanted to see the painting of the naked woman. He could tell, from the harshness of the lines used for the curves of the body, that the artist was a woman. Men painted women in all kinds of soft curves, curves that women never had, but most men never knew because they were afraid to look at women. It took a woman to measure a woman and to know the hardness underneath, and this was a woman's work.

The discovery of the covered-over painting made his day. It was like one of those fine details sometimes found in a corner of a Hieronymus Bosch painting, one of those details that you might overlook the first hundred times you saw the painting, and then on the 101st you would discover it, and the shout of surprise would rise in your throat, and you would not even care that other men had discovered it first. For you, it was your own discovery, real and personal and immediate. It made you a Columbus, and so Hunt felt as he tromped on the gas pedal and sped on.

On further, off the main highway, down into the working-hard-at-it artsy-craftsy towns that gave the north Bay area its bad name among art lovers, and then he was coming over a hill and then down a long grade and then, in a flash, he went from Marin County countryside into outskirt suburbs that could have been picked up and relocated anywhere in the United States, and then he was past that into a town center that was frontierlike and gallery-perfect.

Mill Valley. He drove into the heart of town, past the modernistic lumber store. Stopped for a light at a corner, he could see an old corner pub. In front were three motorcycles with stickers proclaiming that Jesus Saves, and the savings must have been substantial because the bikes were customized Harley Davidson choppers that went for three thousand dollars each.

Another block and Hunt hung a left and began moving his old 1952 MG up a hill that was like riding along the back of a giant snake that had curled up on the roadway to die. And then he was upon the hidden driveway, almost past it, and he yanked the car down into second gear, spun the front wheels to the right to skid the rear end while he jammed the brake, then turned off the car key and released the brake just as the car lined itself up nose-first to go into the driveway, and the car raced ahead, but then slowed down of its own weight, and Hunt folded his arms and let the car roll, and he was not at all surprised when it stopped precisely one inch from a closed garage door.

Unlike civilized America where the garage is either attached to the house or in close proximity to it, the garage hung out over the edge of a cliff, and Hunt saw steps on the side, leading downward.

As he stepped onto the stairs, he was met by four men, large men with inscrutable brown faces, wearing long pink robes. Arms folded, they stared at him.

"I'm Ferdi ..."

123

"We know who you are," said one man. "You will follow us."

Down, two stories below the garage, the house nestled on an outcropping of rock, a gray cedar sprawl surrounded by windows on all sides.

Wordlessly, Hunt was ushered into the house and taken to a small pink room on the second floor of the building. The room resounded with pings. He was pushed inside and saw himself looking at the back of a big metal cabinet that stood in the center of the floor. Jutting out from either side of the cabinet, he could see lightly polished English riding boots and plaid jodphurs.

"He is here, Blissful Master," said a voice behind Hunt.

"Get out, for Christ's sake," came a voice from behind the machine.

Then Hunt was alone. He felt the door close behind him. He heard another set of pings, ping, ping, ping, and then, "Oh, shit."

A fat face peered from around the machine.

"So you're the button man," it said.

"I am Ferdinand De Chef Hunt," said Hunt, who did not know what a button man was and did not know why he was here except that the two owners of his firm had put him on leave of absence with full pay and had paid his way to San Francisco.

"Are you as good as those two Wall Street dingalings say you are?"

Hunt, who did not know, shrugged.

The Maharaji Gupta Mahesh Dor stood up behind the machine. He had been sitting on a high barstool and, standing, he still was not as tall as the machine. He wore brown, red, and white plaid jodphurs, deep brown boots, and a tan T-shirt with three monkeys—hear no evil, see no evil, speak no evil—on it, and the shirt was pulled tight across his soft, almost feminine-breasted chest.

"Grab a stool," he said. "You know what I want?"

"I don't even know who you are," said Hunt, moving to the black leather tufted barstool, matching the one Dor had been sitting on. Dor turned to face him and leaned back against his stool.

"You got a name besides Hunt?"

"Ferdinand De Chef Hunt."

"Okay. Ferdinand it is. You can call me Maharaji or Blissful Master or God, whatever pleases you." He looked at Hunt carefully. "There's trouble in paradise, pal."

"There's always trouble in paradise," said Hunt.

"I'm glad you know that. Then you understand why I need an avenging angel. Is that seraphim or cherubim? I don't know, I can never keep them straight. Theology was never really my bag; business administration was. Anyway, Ferdinand . . ." As he talked, Dor turned toward the electronic ping-pong machine, depressed a red button, and a white dot sprung from one side of the machine and moved slowly across the face of the television screen to the other side. Dor put one hand on a knob on the right, another on the knob on the left, and with a sidelong glance at the machine, intercepted the moving dot by turning the knob and repositioning the small vertical line. The dot seemed to rebound from the small line, back to the other side of the screen. Hunt watched, fascinated.

Dor kept speaking, paying only casual attention to the game. "Anyway," he said, "I got a big number to do here Tuesday night, and two guys are stepping on my skirt. They went to my place in Patna, that's our Pentagon in India, and laid all kinds of shit on my troops. Scared away some of my bodyguards and yanked back one of my broads."

"Who are they?" asked Hunt, still wondering why he had been sent here.

"I'm getting to that." Ping. Ping. Ping. "A week or so ago, one of my defectors was killed. And then one of my troops was killed. And then another one. Right here in the

U.S. of A., which is a drag, man." Ping. Ping. Ping. "Anyway, these guys got killed with crushed necks, and all the old hankie heads with me are moaning and groaning about some kind of curse."

Ping. Ping. Ping.

"It's two guys been doing it, and I figure they're around here somewhere. That's why I'm hiding out here in the hills instead of being in the city."

"So what do you want from me?"

"I don't want these two messing up my number at Kezar Stadium, man. This is the big flagpole toot for my American scene, and I don't need interference."

"What do you want me to do?" asked Hunt.

Dor wheeled on the stool. His hands came off the levers, and there was the ring of a bell as the unintercepted dot hit the far side of the screen and scored a point. Score: 1 to 0, the top of the machine flashed. Dor looked at Hunt.

"Well, I didn't want you to cook them a meal, shmuck. I want you to off them."

Hunt watched the machine again as the white dot reappeared and moved from right to left. Unintercepted, it vanished at the left of the screen. The bell rang. The score changed to 2–0. Hunt could smell the heat from the machine.

"Off them?" he said.

"Yeah. Punch their tickets."

"Punch their tickets?"

"For Jesus' sake, are you stupid or what? Kill them, dummy."

Hunt smiled. So that's what a button man was. As he watched, the score on the untended machine mounted to 3–0, 4–0, 5–0.

"What kind of hit man are you anyway," Dor asked. "How many notches on your piece?"

"By that, I assume you mean how many men have I killed?"

"Righto, Ferdy. How many?"

"None."

Dor looked at him with annoyance creasing his smooth, unlined face. "Wait a minute," he said. "What is this crap?"

Hunt shrugged.

"Goddamit, I asked for a hit man and I get a southern gentleman who sits there like a bump on a log and smirks. What the hell is going on here?"

"I can kill them," Hunt said, and was surprised to hear his voice say that.

"Sure, pal. Sure. I had ninety-eight bodyguards at Patna, a bigger goddam internal security force than old Crossback in Rome, and you know where they are? All ninety-eight? They're back in the hills pissing in their pants, all because of these two creeps. And now you're going to get them? Hah."

Ping, ping, ping. The score was 11–0, and the vertical lines disappeared. The game was over, and the white dot began to move randomly back and forth with none of the intensity of a ball in play.

"I can kill them," Hunt said again, calmly, and this time it sounded more natural to him, as if it were something he should have been saying all his life.

Dor turned back to the machine, waving a hand at Hunt in disgust, in a gesture of go on, get out of here, you bum.

Hunt sat and watched as Dor played the game with grim intensity, playing both sides with both knobs. The score seesawed back and forth, 1–0, 1–1, 2–1, 3–1. Each point took a long time to play and gave Hunt time to think. Why not? His family had done it for centuries. The two stockbrokers, Dalton and Harrow, had talked about Hunt's becoming very wealthy. And why not? Why

127

not? Why not? At that moment, Ferdinand De Chef Hunt returned to the ancestral bosom of his family and decided to become a hit man. And now, goddamit, he was not going to be dissuaded from it by this porky little pig.

"What is that game?" he asked aloud.

"Electronic Ping-Pong," Dor said. "Ever play it?"

"No. But I can beat you."

Dor laughed derisively.

"You couldn't beat me if I wore a blindfold," he said.

"I could beat you if *I* wore a blindfold," said Hunt.

"Get out of here, will you?" said Dor.

"I will play you," said Hunt.

"Go away."

"My life against the job. The game decides."

Dor turned and looked at Hunt's face. The American rose and walked to the machine.

"You're serious, aren't you?" said Dor.

"It's my life," said Hunt. "I don't fool with it."

Dor clapped his hands. The dot went from side to side on the machine. Unhindered, it kept scoring points for the server.

The door opened, and in it stood the four men who had escorted Hunt into the house.

"We're going to play Ping-Pong," said Dor. "If he loses, waste him." He turned to Hunt. "That all right with you?"

"Of course. But what if I win?"

"Then you and I will talk."

"We will talk in the six-figure kind of talk?" Hunt said.

"Right, but don't worry about it. In three minutes, you'll be among the dear departed." He reached for the red button to cancel out the game and start a new one.

"Don't do that," said Hunt.

"What?"

"This game is fine," said Hunt.

"I knew it. I knew it. I knew there was a hitch. You

128

want a spot. Well, I'm not spotting anybody no seven points. It's eight to one, make it nine to one, already."

"I'll take the one point. Play," said Hunt, putting his hand on the knob that controlled the left vertical line. The ball pinged gently from the right lower side of the machine toward him.

"It's your funeral," said the maharaji. "And I mean that."

Hunt slowly turned the knob. The vertical line moved up. He reversed the motion of the knob, and the line moved down. He ignored the dot, which moved uninterrupted off his side of the screen.

"Ten to one," said Dor. "One more point."

"You'll never score it," said Hunt. He had the feel now of the knob. He touched the hard black plastic gently with his hand, his fingers gripping easily into the ridges around the knob, molding into them as if the knob had been designed for his hand alone. He could sense the speed of the vertical line, its motion, the turn necessary to move it top, to move it bottom. Without thought, with his brain divorced from what he did, Hunt knew these things. The next serve came from Dor's side of the screen, aimed at the bottom. Dor smiled. Hunt moved his vertical paddle slowly downward, and as the dot rebounded upward, his paddle intercepted it, and the white dot went straight back across the bottom of the screen. Dor moved his line downward directly in front of the dot and let it rebound straight back, along its approach line, back toward Hunt.

Hunt's vertical line had not moved since he had returned the serve. Now it was in the same position to return the ball straight back across the screen, but as the dot approached the electronic paddle, Hunt moved the vertical line and the movement hit the dot, as if off a curved paddle, sending it up toward the top of the screen. Dor moved his paddle up to intercept it right at the top, forming an upside down L between paddle and top of screen, but the dot slid over the top of his paddle and the machine pinged.

"Ten to two," said Hunt with a smile. He realized there was a dead spot at the top of the machine from which a paddle could not return a ball. Now to see if there was one at the bottom of the screen.

The serve switched to Dor now. The game went on. There was a blind spot in the bottom of the screen too. Ten-three, ten-four, ten-five.

Dor played in growing frustration, shouting at the moving dot. Hunt stood silently alongside the machine, moving his control knob slowly, almost casually.

When the score reached ten–ten, Dor smashed the heel of his pudgy left hand against the base of the machine. On its face, it registered TILT, and the electronic paddles disappeared.

"Okay," he said to the four men, who stood just inside the doorway. "Okay, okay. Bug off."

As they left, Hunt said, "That was right-handed. I haven't shown you left-handed yet."

"Don't bother."

"How about left-handed with a blindfold?"

"You can't play this with a blindfold. How can you play if you don't see?"

"You don't have to see," said Hunt. "You've never noticed. The machine makes a different sound when a ball is coming in low than it does when it's coming in high. You can hear a siss that tells you fast or slow."

"You know, I don't think I like you," said Dor.

"I could beat you by telephone," said Hunt.

Dor looked at him, at the studied insolence in Hunt's eyes, so different from the look of bland confusion that was there when he first entered the room. The maharaji decided he could ignore the challenge in order to harness Hunt's talent. He said:

"One hundred thousand dollars. Kill them both."

"Their names?"

"All we've heard so far is Remo and Chiun. They're probably in San Francisco."

"Too bad for them," said Hunt, and he enjoyed saying it.

CHAPTER THIRTEEN

Today, Remo thought, Joleen was almost human.

She had spent the previous evening sitting quietly, listening intently, as Chiun had gently lectured the girls of the San Francisco Divine Bliss Mission; then late at night she had tried to join Chiun on his sleeping mat in the large bedroom that had been given to Remo and Chiun.

But Chiun had flitted her away with a swish of his hand, and she had settled for Remo and climbed into his bed, and because he was tired and wanted to sleep, Remo serviced her, just so that he did not have to listen to her talk.

The cab episode yesterday had weakened her insane devotion to Maharaji Gupta Mahesh Dor, and their sojourn in bed last night must have weakened her even further, Remo decided, because today she was talking like a human being and not like a recorded announcement.

Chiun, meanwhile, had spent the morning complaining that insects had bothered him all night, while he tried to sleep, and when Remo said they had not bothered him, Chiun had suggested that they would not bother one of their own.

Now they sat in the front seat of a rented car, Joleen sandwiched between Chiun and Remo.

"I do not understand," said Joleen.

"Hear, hear," said Remo.

"If you are a Master," she said, "what then is the maharaji?"

"For small people there are small things," said Chiun. "For large people, there are large things. It is the same with masters."

Joleen did not answer. She clamped her mouth tightly and thought. Chiun looked across her body toward Remo.

"Where are we going?" asked Chiun. "I did not know we could reach Sinanju by automobile."

"We are not going to Sinanju. Now knock it off."

"I think this one is cruel," Joleen said to Chiun, nodding her head toward Remo.

"Ah, how well you know him. See, Remo. She knows you. Cruel."

"Don't forget arrogant," said Remo.

"Yes, child," Chiun said to Joleen. "Do not forget arrogant. Or, for that matter, slothful, inept, lazy, and stupid."

"Yet he is your disciple," she said.

"To make beauty from a diamond is given to many men," said Chiun. "Ah, but to make beauty from a pale piece of pig's ear is something else. That takes the skill of a master. I am still trying to make him seem human. Beauty will come later." He folded his arms.

"Could you make beauty of me?" she said.

"More easily than of him. You have not his bad habits. He is a racist."

"I hate racists," Joleen said. "My father is a racist."

"Ask the racist where we're going," said Chiun.

"Where are we going?"

"I'm taking us out for some fresh air. All that incense and bowing and scraping was getting me down."

"See. He is an ingrate too," Chiun confided. "People willingly open their doors to him, and he downgrades their gift and their hospitality. What an American. If he tells you he will take you back to Patna, do not believe him. White men never keep their promises to others."

"Hey, Chiun. She's as white as I am. She's from Georgia for Christ's sake."

"I don't think I want to go back to Patna anymore," Joleen announced suddenly.

"See," said Chiun. "She is different from you. Already she grows in wisdom, while you have learned less than nothing in the last decade of your years."

Remo pulled the car to the curb. "All right, everybody out. We're going to walk."

"See," said Chiun. "How he orders us about. Oh, perfidy."

Chiun stepped onto the sidewalk and looked around. "Is this Disneyland?" he asked aloud.

Remo, surprised, looked around him. A small carnival to benefit St. Aloysius Roman Catholic Church had been erected on an asphalted parking lot a half-block away.

"Yes," said Remo. "It's Disneyland."

"I forgive you, Remo, for being a racist. I have always wanted to visit Disneyland. Forget everything I said," he told Joleen. "Who brings the Master to Disneyland is not all bad."

"But . . ." Joleen started to speak. Remo took her elbow. "Quiet, kid," he said. "Just enjoy Disneyland." He squeezed. She understood.

Chiun's body meanwhile was moving up and down as if he were jumping in joy, while keeping his feet planted firmly on the sidewalk. His long saffron robe looked like a pillow case into which shots of air were being jetted, causing it to rise, then deflate, rise, then deflate.

135

"I love Disneyland," said Chiun. "How many rides can I go on?"

"Four," said Remo.

"Six," said Chiun.

"Five," said Remo.

"Agreed. Do you have money?"

"Yes."

"Do you have enough?"

"Yes."

"For her too?"

"Yes," said Remo.

"Come, child. Remo is taking us to Disneyland."

"First, I've got to make a phone call."

Ferdinand De Chef Hunt drove slowly back into San Francisco. The city confused him with its mazelike streets that seemed to run from hill to hill and then vanish.

With help he found Union Street and with more help found the building that housed the San Francisco Divine Bliss Mission. If these two targets, this Remo and Chiun, were looking for Dor around San Francisco, they had probably stopped at the mission.

They had.

"They were here. They were here," said the arch-priest Krishna. "He had a badge," he said.

"Where are they now?"

"They just called. They're at a carnival down near Fisherman's Wharf."

"Do they know where Dor is?"

"Man, how could they know? I don't even know."

"If they should return tonight, don't let them know that I was here," said Hunt. "With luck, they won't be returning."

"Am I supposed to be taking orders from you?" asked Krishna.

Hunt extracted a folded piece of paper from his wallet.

Krishna opened it and read the handwritten message from Dor, introducing Hunt as his chief emissary.

"Heavy, man," said Krishna, handing back the note. "Have you seen *him?*"

"Yes."

"Hail to his Blissful perfection."

"Sure, sure, sure. When did they leave?"

"An hour ago. If you see the Blissful Master again, tell him our mission joyously awaits his presence in our city."

"Right. He'll really be impressed," said Hunt.

Hunt went back down the high stone stairs of the building. In a parked car across the street, Elton Snowy watched him carefully.

"What do you think, Elton?" asked one of the two men in the back seat.

"I don't know, Puling, but I think we ought to follow him."

Hunt got into his old MG and pulled smoothly away from the curb.

"Well, then, let's follow him," said Puling. "If it turns out that he's nothing, this here building'll still be here."

"All right," said Snowy, starting the car and pulling into the street.

"Follow that car," giggled Puling. The man next to him let out a Dixie war whoop.

"We gonna stomp that kidnapper," said the man next to Snowy.

Snowy sighed and drove.

Hunt saw the big black car behind him but attached no significance to it. His mind was busy with the prospect of what was ahead, and he felt a pleasurable tingle of anticipation suffuse his entire body. He was on his way to a carnival to do what his family had done so well for so many years, and he looked forward to it. It seemed as if his whole life had been pointed toward just this moment.

"I want to go on the boats."

"You can't go on the boats. That's a kid's ride."

"Tell me where it says that," said Chiun. "Just show me where it says that."

"Right there," Remo said, pointing at a sign. "Kiddy Village. What do you think that means?"

"I don't think it means that I may not ride on the boats."

"Aren't you afraid of looking foolish?" said Remo. He looked toward the boats, four of them, bathtub length, in a circular moat, two feet wide and holding six inches of water. The boats were connected by iron pipes to the motor in the center of the moat. A carnival worker with a dirty, ripped T-shirt and a leather band around his thick right wrist operated the motor from the gate four feet away, at which he also doubled as ticket seller and collector.

"Only a fool looks foolish," said Chiun, "and only a fool twice over worries about it. I want to ride on the boats." He turned toward Joleen. "Tell him I can ride on the boats. You two are both white, maybe you can make him understand."

"Remo, let the Master ride the boat."

"He doesn't want to spend the 25 cents," said Chiun. "I have sometimes seen him waste whole dollars at a time, and he begrudges me 25 cents."

"All right, all right, all right," said Remo. "But we agreed on five rides. This is your fourth."

"Remo, I tell you this as absolute truth. If you let me go on the boat, I won't even ask for the fifth ride."

"Okay," said Remo.

Remo went up to the ticket seller and fished a quarter from his pocket. "One," he said.

The ticket man smiled a gap-toothed grin at Remo. "Sure it won't be too fast for you?"

"It's not for me, sweetheart. Now let's have the ticket

138

before I tell the police of thirteen states that I found you."

"Okay, wiseass," said the ticket man. He ripped a ticket from a thick roll. "Here." He took the quarter.

"Do yourself another favor," said Remo. "When this ticket is used, don't say anything."

"Huh?"

"Don't make any comments and don't try to be a smart-ass. Just do yourself some good and keep your big mouth shut."

"You know, I don't like you. I think I'd like to work you over."

"I know, except you're worried I might be related to your parole officer. Just do what I said. No remarks."

Remo walked away and handed the ticket to Chiun who looked disappointed.

"None for her?"

"She didn't say she wanted one."

"Do you want one, girl? Do not be afraid," said Chiun. "Remo is very rich. He can afford it."

"No, that's all right," she said.

Chiun nodded, then walked toward the "Splashy-Washy," Remo at his side. "I'm kind of glad she didn't want to ride," he confided. "Screaming women annoy me."

Chiun handed his ticket to the ticket taker, who looked at the frail old Oriental, then at Remo. Remo raised his right index finger to his lips, suggesting silence.

"Be sure to fasten your seat belt, papasan," said the ticket taker. "Wouldn't want you falling out and drowning."

"I will. I will," said Chiun. He stepped forward past the ticket taker and walked around the shallow moat. He got into a blue boat, carefully arranging his robes around him on the narrow seat, then quickly got out and walked toward a red boat. Heading toward the red boat at that moment was a five-year-old girl, her face smiling, long golden hair splashing about her face, short dress bobbing up behind her rump as she skipped. Chiun saw her coming and broke into a run.

They reached the red boat at the same time.

Each paused.

Chiun pointed toward the sky. "Look! Look!" he said in a voice of astonishment. "Look up there!"

The little girl followed Chiun's finger and looked up. As her head went up, Chiun darted by her, jumping into the red boat. When the girl looked down, he was already settled in the seat.

Her face wrinkled up, and she seemed about to cry.

"The blue boat is nicer," said Chiun.

"I want to ride in the red boat," she said.

"Go ride in the blue boat."

"But I want to ride in the red boat."

"So do I," said Chiun, "and I got here first. Be gone with you."

The little girl stamped her foot. "Get out of my boat."

Chiun folded his arms across his chest. "Try the blue boat," he said.

"No," she said.

"I will not force you to ride in the blue boat," said Chiun. "You may stand there forever if you wish."

"Get out of my boat," the little girl cried.

"Yeah, old-timer, get out of her boat," said the ticket taker.

Remo tapped the ticket taker on the shoulder. "You forgot already, pal," he said. "Remember what I said? No talk. Do yourself a favor. Butt out."

"I'm running this ride. He should get out of the red boat."

"You going to tell him that?"

"You bet your ass I am," said the ticket taker, standing up.

"Where do you want the remains sent?" asked Remo.

140

The ticket taker stomped off, and took a place alongside the little girl, looking down at Chiun.

"Get out of that boat."

"She can ride in the blue one," said Chiun. "And you can ride in the yellow one."

"She's riding in the red one."

Chiun turned sideways in the seat so he did not have to look at the man's face. "Start the ride," he said. "I'm tired of waiting."

"Not until you get out of there."

Chiun called, "Remo, make him start the ride."

Remo turned his back so no one would know he knew Chiun.

"You whites all stick together," grumbled Chiun.

"No snotty cracks either," said the ticket taker. "If you don't like this country, go back where you came from."

Chiun sighed and turned. "That is good advice. Why don't you follow it?"

"This is where I came from."

"No, it is not," said Chiun. "Does not your book say, 'From dust you came, to dust you go'?"

Remo heard that and turned in time to see Chiun rise up in his seat, his saffron robe swirling about him. Before Remo could move, the ticket taker was spread-eagled across the bow of the small fiberglass boat, his face under the water.

"Chiun, knock it off already," said Remo, moving toward the boat.

"That's right, take his side," said Chiun, still holding the flailing man's head under water.

"Let him go, Chiun," called Remo.

"No."

"Okay, that's it," said Remo. "No more rides." He turned his back.

"Wait, Remo. Wait. See. I let him go. See. He is all

141

right. See. Tell him you're all right." Chiun slapped the man's face. "Stop your stupid choking, and tell him you are all right."

The ticket taker caught his breath and pulled back from Chiun in fright. He looked at Remo who shrugged an I-told-you-so shrug. "Better start the ride," he said.

The ticket taker went back to his chair and turned the knob to the on position. The engine chugged and the boat started. The five-year-old shouted in anger. Remo took a dollar bill from his pocket and handed it to her. "Here," he said. "Go buy yourself some ice cream, and you can have the red boat on the next ride."

The girl snatched the bill from Remo's hand and raced away. Chiun's boat floated gently past Remo. "I see you got rid of that sniveling little wretch," he said. "Good for you."

"Better make it a long ride," said Remo as he walked back past the ticket taker, to rejoin Joleen.

By the time Ferdinand De Chef Hunt reached the amusement park, he was sure the black car behind him was following him. So he carefully parked his car in a restaurant driveway a block from the carnival, darted into the side door of the restaurant, through the dining room, and out the door on the other side of the building.

He carefully made his way along the wooden and concrete piers for another half block until he was opposite the carnival. Glancing behind him, he saw no sign of his pursuers and walked casually across the street toward the park.

Now to find those two men, what were their names? . . . Remo and Chiun.

Chiun leaned over the wooden railing and carefully rolled a nickel off his fingertips. It arced forward, turning over exactly one revolution, then landed absolutely flat on a platform slightly raised above the asphalt floor. The nickel stopped in the direct center of a small red circle, one of hundreds of red circles painted on a large piece of white linoleum. The circles were only slightly larger in diameter than a nickel. A player won a prize if his nickel landed fully on a red circle, and did not overlap into the white border.

"Another winner," called Chiun.

The concession operator looked skyward as if asking for mercy.

"This time I want the pink rabbit," said Chiun. Behind him stood Remo and Joleen, their arms filled with plush toys, small games, stuffed animals. Remo precariously dangled a goldfish bowl, complete with occupant, from the fingers of his right hand.

The operator took a small pink stuffed rabbit from a shelf in the rear of the booth and handed it to Chiun. "Okay, here you are. Now why not go someplace else?"

"Why not is because I want to play this game," said Chiun.

"Yeah, but you're wiping me out," said the operator. "You've won nineteen prizes in a row."

"Yes, and I'm going to win more."

"Not here, you're not," said the operator, his voice rising with his temper.

Chiun spoke over his shoulder. "Remo, talk to him. Threaten to report him to Mr. Disney."

"Why don't we leave?" said Remo.

"You don't want to see me win either," said Chiun. "You're jealous."

"Right. I'm jealous. All my life, I've wanted my own goldfish, three yellow rubber duckies, seven stuffed pussycats, a plastic checker game, and two armfuls of slum."

The operator looked up at Remo, recognizing "slum" as the in-carnival word for junk prizes.

He looked at Remo questioningly. Remo nodded and

winked as if sharing a fraternity secret. The operator understood now. Remo was a hustler, preparing to pluck this old yellow pigeon. He nodded back imperceptibly.

"Sure, old man," the operator said. "Go right ahead."

"Watch this, Remo," said Chiun. "I will do it with my eyes closed." He screwed his eyes tightly shut. "Are you watching, Remo?"

"Yes, Little Father."

"Can you see me?"

"Yes. Your eyes are closed, not mine."

"Good. Now watch."

Chiun leaned forward over the railing, his eyes shut tightly. He flipped the nickel off the fingernail of his right thumb, high into the air, almost up to the canvas roof over the game. The nickel spun rapidly, flipping all the way up, flipping all the way down, made one final turn, and landed flat on its side, directly in the center of a red circle.

Chiun kept his eyes closed. "I can't look. I can't look. Did I win?"

Remo nodded toward the nickel. The concession operator put his toe on it and slid it off the red spot, half onto the white.

"No, you lose," said Remo.

Chiun opened his eyes in shock. "You lie," he said. He looked at the nickel, half on the red, half on white. "You cheated me," he said.

"What's worse," said Remo, "you have to give back all the prizes."

"Never. Never will I part with my goldfish."

"All except the goldfish," said Remo. He gave the operator back the prizes he and Joleen held. The operator happily put them back on the shelf. Remo still held the goldfish bowl.

"You cheated," said Chiun, surprisingly even-voiced. "Tell me the truth. You cheated, didn't you?"

"Yes."

"Why?"

"Because we don't need all that junk."

"I agree. You may need your arms free." Chiun's eyes were narrowed, and he seemed to be sniffing the air.

"What's wrong?" asked Remo.

"Nothing," said Chiun, "yet. Don't drop the goldfish."

When he saw the young white man holding the prizes and the elderly Oriental leaning over the nickel toss game, Ferdinand De Chef Hunt knew. He knew that these were his targets. He felt a strange sensation in his throat, a lump of flesh that would not go up or down. It was a new feeling: Was it the feeling that generations of De Chefs had felt when they were on the prowl?

While they played, Hunt stopped at a booth across the way. He paid a quarter and was handed three baseballs. He had to knock six wooden bottles from the top of a barrel. Hunt backed off and tossed the first ball underhand. The operator smiled. Like a fairy, he thought. The ball hit the center bottom bottle, knocked all bottles to the top of the barrel. The ball skidded around, bumping against bottles, and knocking all of them off onto the ground.

The operator stopped smiling when Hunt did the same thing with his second ball. He glanced over his shoulder and saw the two targets and the girl in the pink sari moving away. He tossed the third ball softly toward the concession stand operator.

"Your prizes," the operator said.

"Keep them," said Hunt, following the three at a stroller's pace.

He let them get twenty yards ahead of him. They were heavy into conversation, but he knew they had not realized that he was following them.

145

In fact, the conversation was, from Chiun's standpoint, much more important.

"I only had four rides," Chiun said. "You promised me five."

"You said if I let you ride the boat, you wouldn't ask for the fifth ride."

"I don't remember saying that," said Chiun. "And I remember everything I say. Why would I say I would be satisfied with four rides when you promised me five? Can you think of a reason I would say that?"

"I give up," said Remo.

"Good," said Chiun. "There's the ride I want to go on." He pointed ahead of them toward "The Flying Bucket," then leaned to Joleen. "You can ride with me. Remo will pay for it."

"Anything you say," said Remo wearily. With Chiun leading the way, the three walked into a narrow corridor between concession booths, toward "The Flying Bucket," a Ferris wheel type of ride in which riders sat in a plastic bucket, attached to an overhead wheel by two steel cables.

As they turned the corner, Hunt lost sight of them. He walked faster toward the corridor they had entered.

Just then, he felt a hand on his shoulder. He turned to look into a red-fatted angry face. Behind it stood four other equally red, equally angry faces.

"Here he is, boys," said Elton Snowy. "Here's the kidnapper now. Where's my daughter?"

Hunt recognized the man as the driver of the black car that had followed him from Divine Bliss headquarters. He shrugged. "I don't know what you're talking about. You must have the wrong man."

"Don't lather me with that, sonny," said Snowy. He grabbed Hunt's arm tightly. The other three men moved up, also grabbing Hunt, and quickly they pushed him between tents into a surprisingly quiet grassy area, deserted of people, yet only a dozen feet from the main midway.

146

"I don't know anything about your daughter, sir," said Hunt again. He would not spend too much time here; he did not want to lose track of his targets.

"Boys, what do you say we work him over to loosen his tongue?" said Snowy.

The four men lunged into Hunt and bore him to the ground with their weight.

Two were on his legs, and two more on his arms, pressing them down into the mushy turf.

"Now we make the sumbitch talk," said Snowy.

The fingers of Hunt's left hand snaked out and curled around one of the triangular metal stakes used to anchor a tent rope. With his fingertips he plucked it from the ground and curled it into his palm. He felt his face being slapped from side to side.

"Talk, you kidnapping bastard. What you doing at that Blissy Mission? Where's my little girl?"

Hunt's right fingers scratched at the ground. He came up with a handful of dirt and a rock the size of a grape. He let the dirt trickle through his fingers.

"It's all a mistake. I don't even know your daughter."

Snowy, who had been holding down Hunt's left arm, while slapping him, now released the arm with a cry of rage and sprung with both hands toward Hunt's throat to strangle the truth from him.

His arm freed, Hunt whizzed the tent peg through the air, catapulting it with just a flip of the wrist.

"Aaargh," came a scream from behind Snowy. He turned to look. The man anchoring Hunt's left leg had a tent peg driven deep into his right bicep. It seemed as if an artery had been severed. Blood stained the man's white short-sleeved shirt and pulsed out of the wound with each heartbeat. Horrified, the man grasped his right arm with his left hand and staggered to his feet.

At almost the same instant, the grape-sized stone curled off Hunt's fingertips. It whistled through the air, then

147

struck the left eye of the man holding Hunt's right leg. The man shouted and fell back heavily, both hands clutching his face.

Snowy, confused, then angry, turned back and plunged downward with both hands toward Hunt's neck. But both legs and the left arm of the intended victim were now free. He rolled his body to the right. Snowy's hands drove into the dirt. At the same moment, Hunt again filled his right hand with dirt and flipped it upward into the face of the man still holding onto his right arm. The man coughed and gagged and released his grip, and Hunt rolled to the right, curled his legs up and flipped up into a standing position.

The bleeding man was in a state of shock. The man hit by the stone still knelt, both hands over his face. The third man was still trying to cough the dirt from his lungs. Snowy knelt on the ground as if terrorizing an invisible victim. But the victim was behind him, and now he put a foot against Snowy's butt and pushed. Hard. Snowy sprawled face forward into the earth.

"Last time," said Hunt. "I don't know your daughter. If you ever bother me again, you won't live to tell about it."

He brushed himself off and walked away, hoping that his intended victims had not escaped him. Behind him, Elton Snowy looked at Hunt's back, groped in his mind for something to shout, something to say that could show the frustration and rage he felt at that moment. His lips moved. Mentally, he rejected words without knowing he did. Then finally he spoke, more of a hiss than a shout: "Nigger lover."

Ferdinand DeChef Hunt heard the words behind him and laughed.

"Whee," said Chiun.
"Whee," said the pretty blond girl with him.

148

And "wheeze" went the twin cables holding up their fiberglass bucket as it slowly turned upward on the converted Ferris wheel superstructure.

"Let us spin the bucket," said Chiun, his eyes alight in merry excitement.

"Let us not spin the bucket," said the girl. "They do not allow us to spin the bucket."

"That is not nice of Mr. Disney," said Chiun. "Why does he have this nice bucket and not allow people to spin it?"

"I don't know," said the girl. "There is a sign down there that says do not spin the bucket."

"Oh," said Chiun.

"Oh," said the girl.

"Oh, oh," said Chiun.

"Oh, oh," said the girl.

"Funny, funny, Mr. Disney," said Chiun. "Wheeee," he added.

Finger hooked in the goldfish bowl, Remo waited patiently below for the ride to end. His attention was fixed upward. Behind him stood Ferdinand De Chef Hunt. His pockets held nothing to use as a weapon. He looked on the ground, but it was asphalted and there was not a stone, not even a pebble he could use.

Hunt turned. Behind him was a concession booth, "The Discus Throw." For a dollar, a player got four thin metal plates, and the chance to scale them frisbee-like through a small hole in the back of the tent. Two plates through won a prize, but few won because the plates were not uniform, and a toss that would send one plate through the hole would send another plate flying skyward toward the roof of the tent.

Hunt pulled a clump of bills from his shirt pocket and tossed them on the counter, grabbing three plates in his left hand.

"I want to buy these," he told the operator, who

149

shrugged. The plates cost him ten cents each. Hunt turned and began walking slowly toward Remo, whose eyes were still staring upward. It would be simple. First the white man, and, then, when he came down, the yellow man.

One plate for each. And a spare. No way to miss.

He was twelve feet from Remo now. Another step. He was ten feet away.

Up above, Chiun had stopped "wheee"ing. He saw the man move toward Remo. His eyes narrowed into slits. There was something wrong; he could feel it; just as he had felt before that someone was following them. But then the Ferris wheel spun up over the top and the wheel assembly was between Chiun and Remo, and he could see Remo no more.

Remo relaxed. The ride was slowing down. It would soon be over. Then he sensed movement behind his right shoulder. He turned casually.

Flashing at him, like a flying saucer, was a metal plate. It spun, noiselessly, at his head, directly on a plane with the ground, its hard cutting edge moving straight for his two eyes.

Damn, and here he was with a goldfish bowl that he couldn't let get broken. The best he could do was slip his head to the right. His left arm crooked at the elbow, and then his hand shot forward like a spear. Its hardened fingertips caught the center of the plate just before it buzzed against his head. The plate shuddered, its metal center crumpled, and dropped at Remo's feet.

Now he looked up. Ten feet away, he saw a thin young man holding two more plates. Remo smiled. He had called the Divine Bliss Mission to let them know where he was, just so that anyone sent by the Maharaji Dor would be able to find him.

Hunt smiled and waited as Remo moved another step closer. The fool. By chance, he had gotten his hand up and stopped the first plate. He would not be lucky this time.

Another step by Remo, who was being very careful and moving slowly, so as not to spill any water from the goldfish bowl.

The plate in Hunt's right hand curled back under his left elbow, then shot forward toward Remo's throat. At eight feet it could not miss.

But, damn it, he was lucky again. He caught the edge of the plate, sliding off his left wrist, and the plate spun off its course, down into the asphalt pavement, where it dug a six-inch-long gouge before stopping.

Remo took another step forward. Hunt realized plates would not do. He needed a sturdier weapon, and he had no stomach for hand-to-hand combat. He heard another "whee" from the Flying Bucket.

Time to split.

He looked up. The car carrying the Oriental had reached the bottom point of the ride and was now on its way up again. Hunt's right hand again snaked back under his left elbow and then sent the third plate silently screaming toward the ride. Remo turned to watch, then moved toward the ride. The plate flew toward the car Chiun and Joleen occupied. Its front edge bit through the thin steel cable holding up the right side of the car, hacked through it, before the plate clattered off the side of the car toward the ground.

The car started to drop.

"Wheeee," said Chiun, giggling. His left arm reached up and grabbed the frayed strand of cable. His left toe found a crevice inside the car and hooked itself into it. His right hand grabbed the safety bar. His left hand overhead, and his left foot and right hand below, prevented the car from plunging, and still shouting "wheeee" with all his might, Chiun held the car together as it rode up,

151

around, and over the top of the wheel, with Joleen huddling in panic on her side of the compartment.

"Stop that damned thing," Remo yelled at the operator, who instantly pushed the heavy lever that tossed in the clutch of the motor, then squeezed the hand grip that acted as a brake. When the cars came around, the operator saw the broken cable and the old Oriental holding the car together. Expertly the operator brought the ride to a stop just as Chiun's car reached the wooden boarding platform. Chiun released his left hand grip on the cable. The car dropped four inches and settled against the wooden platform.

Chiun's face was framed in a smile. "Wheeeee," he said. He jumped out of the car. "What a wonderful ride. Do you have my goldfish?"

"Yes, I have it. You all right?"

Chiun smirked and looked toward Joleen, recovering from her shock and rising slowly to her feet.

"Of course, we're all right," he said. "These rides are safe. No one ever gets hurt. Mr. Disney would not let that happen."

Remo turned. The young man had gone. Following him now would be a waste of time.

Later, outside the carnival, Chiun confided, "There is one thing, Remo, I do not understand."

"What's that?"

"When Mr. Disney shoots the plate at the cable and breaks it, how many people have the control to grip the cable and hold the vehicle together? Do not some fall?"

"No," said Remo, his right index finger hooked into the goldfish bowl. "That's the first thing we Americans learn. How to grab the cable and hold the ride together."

"A very curious thing," said Chiun. "Here you are, a nation of people who cannot talk and cannot run and cannot move well, who eat the flesh of every sort of beast, and yet you can do that."

"It is easy," said Remo.

"Another thing. Did you see someone following you in the park? A thin, young man?"

"No," said Remo. "I didn't see anybody."

"Typical," said Chiun. "You never notice anything. Don't drop the goldfish."

CHAPTER FOURTEEN

Although he fled the amusement park, Hunt had a smile on his face that would have been hard to ascribe to failure.

The young American had been able to block the plates, and Hunt would no longer call it luck. So this Remo was exceptional. So? So it did not matter. Hunt had been warned years before by his grandfather that there were some such people.

In recollection now, it seemed as if his grandfather had been trying to prepare him for the life of the assassin, but that too was immaterial. What was important was that his grandfather had told him of the way to deal with people who had physical skills that were out of the ordinary. A simple technique, but foolproof. Next time, there would be no swift hands blocking plates.

Hunt smiled again as he drove out toward the lower edge of San Francisco and the Golden Gate Bridge. He knew how he would handle this Remo the next time they met, and he looked forward to the meeting.

Meanwhile, Elton Snowy had other things on his mind.

He stood at the counter of the sporting goods store on Market Street.

"I want a gross of shells. Double O buck."

"A gross?" asked the clerk, smiling faintly.

"A gross. That's one hundred forty and four."

"Yes, sir. Big hunting trip, eh?"

"You might say that," said Snowy. He paid cash and angrily signed his real name and address to the register kept in the gun department. The clerk noted the name as Snowy left the shop, then, recalling the look of grim anger on the big man's red face, walked toward the telephone.

Snowy's next stop was another sporting goods store at the farthest end of Market Street, where the street dissolves into a maze of crossing streets and highways and trolley tracks, seemingly always under repair. There he purchased a .38 caliber revolver and ammunition, again paid cash, again signed a register, and again, a clerk, noting the set to his jaw, waited until the man had left and then called the police department.

Snowy's last stop was a bar across the street from a railroad yard, where he drank bourbon, struck up a conversation with a drunken off-duty switchman, and finally wound up buying a dozen railroad detonating caps for fifty dollars cash.

While no report of that transaction reached the police, the first two reports had set them in motion. Two city detectives got a description of Snowy but could not find him registered in any motel, because by now Snowy was in a furnished room under an assumed name, carefully opening shotgun shells and pouring the powder into a plastic bag.

The detectives dutifully reported their failure to find Snowy. Their report went to the detective commander and was routinely picked up by an FBI messenger. The agent-in-charge of the San Francisco office read the report. Nor-

156

mally, he would have flipped it into an outbasket full of other inconsequential matters. But today was different.

For the past week, there had been a highest-priority order that any unusual activity in arms buying should be reported cross-channels to the CIA in Virginia, just outside Washington, D.C. The agent-in-charge did not know why; he suspected it had something to do with that guru coming to San Francisco and the CIA wanting to avoid an international incident, but it was no real business of his until someone told him it was a real business of his.

He picked up the safe line and called Washington.

A house in Mill Valley, across the bay from San Francisco, resounded with "Ping. Ping. Ping. Ping."

"'In other words, you failed," said Maharaji Gupta Mahesh Dor.

Hunt smiled and shook his head. "In other words, I sized them up. They're tough, that's all."

"I tell you, man, I'm not going to put my ass in a sling by having any Bliss rally with those two nuts around."

For a moment, he looked like a frightened little boy.

Hunt rose from his chair and put a hand on the fat teenage shoulder. "Don't worry about it," he said. "I'll be there. If either or both of them come, they're gone. That's it."

Blaring in the corner of the room was a television set. The announcer's voice cut into the automatically ignored music of the singing commercial with a bulletin: "Three men wounded in an outbreak of violence at an amusement park. Details at six o'clock."

Dor turned to Hunt. "You?" he asked.

Hunt nodded. "They were bugging me."

The Blissful Master looked at Hunt's cold face for a moment, then smiled. "All systems go, man. We're gonna bliss 'em to death tomorrow night."

CHAPTER FIFTEEN

The reports on Elton Snowy's ammunition purchases were, within hours, on the desk of the high CIA official who had asked for them.

His name was Cletis Larribee and he was fifty-one years old and a native of Willows Landing, Tennessee, where he had been for many years elder and Sunday deacon and lay preacher and president of the Men's Club of the Monumental Baptist Church.

Larribee had failed to distinguish himself with the OSS during World War II and had also failed to distinguish himself during postwar service with the fledgling intelligence operation that was a spinoff of the wartime OSS and would someday grow up to be the CIA. He had further failed to distinguish himself by never getting into any trouble, and this had so distinguished him in latterday Washington that when the post of number two man at the CIA had opened up, the then president had said, "Put that Bible-thumping characterization omitted in charge. At least we know he won't expletive deleted up."

Cletis Larribee had no intention of expletive deleting up. He wanted to serve America, even if sometimes America

159

did not seem to want serving. It was becoming godless and revolutionary, casting aside old values, with nothing to replace them. Cletis Larribee never cast aside old values without replacing them with something.

It fell into Larribee's province to know that the Maharaji Gupta Mahesh Dor was in the United States to hold a Blissathon, and as he had explained to his superior, "All we need is to have this holy man knocked off in America, what with the state of the world and all," and that argument had won him the right to get domestic police reports on arms purchases in San Francisco, and now he studied the Elton Snowy reports with deep and growing worry.

He decided to call a friend of his, a high official in the FBI, for advice, but his friend's secretary told him that the FBI official was in the hospital. "Oh, no, nothing serious. Routine checkup, that's all."

Larribee telephoned another close friend in the State Department, India desk.

"I'm sorry, Mr. Larribee, but Mr. Volz is in the hospital. No. Nothing serious. Just his usual physical."

Three hospitalized friends later, Cletis Larribee began to suspect that something might be wrong. He confided this to his two closest friends at lunch at an inexpensive restaurant outside Washington, D.C. Perhaps the maharaji's life was in danger, he felt.

"Nonsense," said Winthrop Dalton.

"Double nonsense," said V. Rodefer Harrow III. "Nothing can imperil the Blissful Master's plans."

"He is truth," said Dalton.

"He is perfect truth," said Harrow, not wishing to be outdone.

"He is mortal," said Larribee, "and he can die at the hands of an assassin."

"Nonsense," said Dalton.

"Double nonsense," said V. Rodefer Harrow III. "The Master's security arrangements are like he is. Perfect."

"But against an assassin with a bomb?" said Larribee.

"I am not at liberty to discuss them," said Dalton, "but the security arrangements are more than adequate. We made them ourselves." He looked to Harrow for reassurance.

"Right," said Harrow. "Made 'em ourselves." He signaled the waiter to bring another free tray of cellophane-wrapped cheese crackers, one of the reasons he had always liked this restaurant.

"Maybe I should alert the FBI," said Larribee.

"No," said Dalton. "You should simply follow instructions and be at Kezar Stadium tomorrow night—prepared to show America the right way. Do you have everything you need?"

Larribee nodded and glanced down at his tan leather briefcase. "I've got it all. Cuba. Chile. Suez Canal. Spain. The whole works."

"Good," said Dalton. "When America sees you join with the Blissful Master, all America will flock to his side."

"And don't worry," said Harrow. "The Blissful Master is protected by God."

Larribee smiled. "The Blissful Master *is* God."

Dalton and Harrow looked at him, and after a pause Dalton said, "Yes, he is, isn't he?"

And three hundred miles north of Washington, D.C., in a sanitarium on the shores of Long Island Sound, Dr. Harold W. Smith read a sheaf of reports that failed to quell his uneasiness.

The highly placed people that Remo had named to him as followers of the maharaji had been placed into hospitals, at least until Dor had left the country.

But there might be more, and Smith had no line on

who they were or what they might be planning. Add to that the absolute blank drawn so far on the maharaji's whereabouts. Add again Remo's report that someone had tried to kill him that day in San Francisco.

The sum total was trouble. The "big thing," whatever it was, was coming, and Smith felt powerless. Not only could he not stop it, he couldn't even identify it, and right now his only hope was Remo.

CHAPTER SIXTEEN

The sun was at 12 o'clock high when two Indian men wearing pink robes, a pudgy fat Indian woman in a pink robe and a veil wrapped tightly around her head, and a thin young American man arrived at the back gate of Kezar Stadium.

They showed some identification to a uniformed guard, who quickly waved them through the turnstile and pointed them to a ramp thirty feet away.

The foursome went up the ramp, then down stone stairs into the playing surface of Kezar Stadium. They carefully checked the bandstand platform, which had been erected in the center of the stadium, poking around under it. Then, apparently satisfied, they walked across the field and up another ramp that led to locker rooms and a suite of offices.

They passed through a door that read "Absolutely No Admittance" and into a suite of offices. Inside, the pudgy young Indian woman said, "Shit, this is hot," and began to strip off her robe.

When the robe was off, the woman was a woman no

longer. Wearing the disguise had been Maharaji Gupta Mahesh Dor, and now he was resplendent in a white satin suit with pants that were gathered and puffed out from hip to knee, then wrapped tightly about his calves, and a Nehru jacket with a jeweled collar.

He shook himself, as if trying to detach himself from his sticky hotness.

"Hey, you, what's your name?" he shouted to one of the middle-aged Indian men who bore silver stripes down their foreheads. "Go outside and see if you can find that television shmuck. He's supposed to meet us here at twelve."

He turned to go into an inner office. The young American followed. At the doorway, Dor said over his shoulder: "And you, Ferdinand, keep your eyes open for those troublemakers. I don't want to have to leave here in disguise too."

Ferdinand De Chef Hunt smiled. His teeth shone pearly white, as white as the two perfectly round white stones he manipulated in the fingers of his right hand, the two stones, one of which he knew would be blood red before the evening was over.

The inner office was a small, remorselessly air-conditioned room, with only overhead lighting and no windows.

"This'll do," said Dor, plopping himself into a chair behind the large wooden desk.

"I have found him, O Blissful One," came an Indian voice from the door. Dor looked up and saw the Indian man leading in a tweedy young man with bushy red hair and glasses.

"Good, now everybody split. I want to talk to this guy for a while. About tonight."

"Tonight will be a night of beauty, Blissful Master," said the Indian.

"Yeah, sure. Tell me again about the cume potential," he said to the television man. "What can we grab on just one network, live, catching both coasts?"

"We will catch the spirit of all those who seek after truth," the Indian man spoke again.

"Will you get the hell out of here with your drivel? I've got business to talk about. Well?" he said again to the television man.

"Actually, we envision that your program slot will fit neatly into the gap between . . ."

Hunt smiled again and followed the Indian out of the room, closing the door behind him. Television merchandising did not interest him. Only killing did.

Although the program was not to begin until 8 p.m., the crowd began arriving at 5 o'clock. They were mostly young, mostly hairy, mostly intense, although there were more than a few who smuggled in their own secular bliss devices in paper bags in hip pockets, or in tightly rolled joints stashed into the corners of regular cigarette packs.

Another early arrival carried a bag, but it did not contain bliss. Elton Snowy walked through the entry turnstile and up the steps into the stadium, then downstairs to get as close as possible to the bandstand. In his right arm he carried a large bag, the top of which showed a pile of pieces of fried chicken. Under the chicken was a plastic bag filled with gunpowder, steel filings, and the highly explosive heads of railroad detonating caps.

Snowy moved down the steps toward the first row of seats. Against his left leg he felt the uncomfortable thumping of the .38 caliber pistol he had taped to his leg. He didn't know if a pistol shot would detonate his homemade bomb, but he was going to try it. Unless he found Joleen first. He squeezed his bag grimly, as if resisting an invisible attempt to remove it from him.

Remo, Chiun, and Joleen were late arrivals, it being well after dusk when they entered Kezar Stadium.

Chiun's luggage from San Diego had finally arrived at the San Francisco hotel suite Remo had rented, and Chiun had insisted upon watching his beautiful dramas, which is what he called afternoon television soap operas. He would not hear of leaving before they were over, unless, of course, Remo wanted to take him again to Disneyland and the fun ride in the Flying Bucket.

Since that was the thing Remo wanted to do least in the world, they waited, and it was only after the last TV serial was over that Chiun rose from the floor, his red robe swirling about him, and said: "We will never get to Sinanju by waiting here."

Inside the stadium, they found a madhouse. The crowd was small in comparison to the size of the stadium, only 15,000 people. The Divine Bliss followers sat close in, in the box seats and the infield folding chairs, distinguishable instantly by their pink robes and the look of the zealot in their eyes. But that was only half the crowd. The other half consisted of curiosity seekers, troublemakers, motorcycle gangs, and they roamed the higher reaches of the stadium, mugging the unwary, fighting with each other, and slowly, systematically destroying stadium equipment.

And over all this confusion rose the raucous voices of a singing group, six men and a girl, who were souling their way through old down-home gospel classics, whose lyrics had been revised to substitute Master or Blissful Master for Jesus.

At least one of the parties was delighted. Maharaji Gupta Mahesh Dor sat in the small office with the television representative, snapping his fingers and saying over and over, "Cool. Cool. That's the way we do it. Cool."

"It reminds me somewhat of Billy Graham," said the
166

earnest young TV man, watching the closed circuit screen that flickered ghostly green in the darkened office.

"Don't knock Billy Graham," said the maharaji. "He's got a nice set. The man's beautiful."

Dor glanced at his watch. "The speakers'll start soon. They're cued for forty-five minutes. Then we start the broadcast, it picks up with my being introduced by one of those nigger Baptists, and then I go on and do my number."

"That's it. That's the schedule," said the TV man.

"Beautiful," said Dor. "You can split now. Go make sure your cameramen take their lens caps off or whatever it is you people do."

Remo left Chiun and Joleen in the playing field section of the stadium to which Chiun's red robes and Joleen's pink sari won them easy admittance. The first speaker was on, a Baptist minister explaining how he had given up false Christianity for the service of a greater good, the work of the Blissful Master. It would have taken very sharp eyes to notice, as the minister waved his arms above his head, that his wrists were faintly scarred.

"That man has been shackled," said Chiun to Joleen.

"He was in Patna," Joleen said, noncommittally.

"Your master is an evil person," said Chiun.

Joleen looked at Chiun and smiled softly. "But he is my master no more. I have a new master." Tenderly she squeezed Chiun's hand, which he flickingly removed from hers.

Meanwhile, Remo made a wrong turn and found himself on the wrong side of the stadium, trying to wend his way along corridors, which generally became boarded over and closed. But all stadiums are alike, and there are always rooms and offices through which one can piece his way to get past roadblocks.

Remo paused in one office to stop a rape, and because

167

he did not have a lot of time, he prevented the rape in the simplest way possible, by rendering the offending instrument harmless.

Then he was back into the corridors, darting into and through offices, and finally he was on the far side of the stadium, trotting along a corridor that led to a ramp that led to the bandstand.

He turned the corner. Ahead of him he saw a door marked "Absolutely No Admittance" and two burly men in pink robes standing in front of it with arms folded.

Remo approached the men.

"Hi, fellas," he said. "Nice day, wasn't it?"

They did not speak.

"A perfect day," said Remo. "For bananafish."

They remained silent, not deigning to look at him.

"All right, boys, move aside," said Remo. "I've got to talk to the swami."

A sharp voice came from behind Remo. "First me," and Remo turned and saw the young American from the carnival.

"Oh, yeah, you," Remo said. "Did you bring your plates?"

"I won't need them," said Ferdinand De Chef Hunt, moving a few steps closer, until only fifteen feet separated him and Remo.

Inside the closed door, Maharaji Dor checked his watch again, looked at the monitor, and saw the network symbol flash on. Time to go. At these rates, he couldn't afford to waste any time.

He stuck his head through the door into the next office, where Winthrop Dalton and V. Rodefer Harrow III sat with Cletis Larribee.

"Everything ready here?" he said.

"Yes, Blissful Master," said Dalton.

Larribee nodded.

"Okay. I'm going out now. You be in the wings in ten minutes."

Dor went back into the office, closed the door, and went through the other door onto a private ramp that led up into a dugout in the infield.

Hunt took the two small stones from his pocket as he faced Remo.

"Plates. Now stones," said Remo. "When do you graduate to pies?"

Hunt only smiled. He positioned the two stones carefully on his palm and fingertips. It was as his grandfather had shown him. The old man had described it to young Ferdinand in terms of animals, but now Hunt knew the old man was talking about people.

"There are some animals that are different from others," the old man had told him. "They're stronger. They're faster. Sometimes they're smarter."

"And how do you bring them down?" the young boy had asked.

"You do it by using their own powers against them." The old man had stood up and gestured toward the woods. "Did you see him?"

"Who?" asked the boy.

"There's a wild boar out there. Tough, fast, mean and smart. He knows we're here, and he's just waiting for us to move on so he can move on."

"So what do you do, grandpa?"

The old man picked up a rifle, then looked around the porch until he found a small stone.

"Watch," he said.

He tossed the stone high into the air, far to the left of the spot where he had seen the boar. The stone came down easily onto a patch of grass, but the boar's supersensitive hearing picked up the sound, and the animal bolted, to the right, away from the sound of the stone. His flight took him past a slim break in the trees, and as his body passed the opening, Grandpa De Chef put a bullet in the beast's head.

"That's how, Ferdie," the old man said. "You make the target commit itself to an empty threat. And then when it's committed, you make the kill." He smiled down at the boy. "Maybe you don't understand it now, but someday you will. No matter what your momma says."

"Come on, pal, I don't have all night." Remo's voice brought Hunt back to where he was.

Without hesitating, without analysis, he brought his right arm back and then fired it forward at Remo. The stone on his fingertips leaped from his hand first, moving toward Remo but two inches to the left of Remo's head.

The second stone, propelled from the palm of Hunt's hand, was only a foot behind, aimed toward Remo's right, so when he ducked away from the first stone, the second would catch him squarely between the eyes.

Hunt smiled, and then the smile changed to astonishment, and then fear.

There was a thud ahead of him and a scream. The first stone had passed Remo's head and buried itself into the forehead of one of the pink-robed guards who stood behind Remo. The man screamed and crumpled.

Remo had not moved a fraction of an inch, and the second stone moved toward the right side of his head, outside the intended target line, and then Remo flicked up his right hand and caught the stone in the air between thumb and forefinger.

Remo looked at the stone, then back at Hunt.

"Sorry, pal. I told you, you should've stuck to plates."

Hunt backed away. "You're going to kill me, aren't you?"

"That's the biz, sweetheart."

Hunt turned and ran down the ramp, toward the brightly lit stadium, and Remo took a few steps after him, then saw up ahead of him the television cameras grinding away.

He stopped. He could not chance being seen on television. Hunt now was in the infield, running toward the bandstand. He glanced once back over his shoulder as he ran.

At that moment, Maharaji Gupta Mahesh Dor stood inside the dugout, shielded from view by a cordon of pink-robed men.

Remo waited, and Hunt turned again. This time, Remo let fly the stone in his right hand. Hunt saw it coming at him, threw up his right hand to block it, and the stone smashed into his hand, cracking the fingers with the force of a hammer, and driving the stone and flesh and finger-bone into Hunt's forehead.

Hunt fell. Two persons who saw him fall screamed, but suddenly their screams were overwhelmed by the roar of the faithful, as the maharaji stepped from the dugout and trotted lightly across the field toward the bandstand.

"Blissful Master. Blissful Master." The stadium resounded with the screams. Hunt's already dead body lay partially under the back of the bandstand, and the two persons who had seen him fall convinced themselves they were mistaken and joined the chanting for Dor.

Remo turned back to the door. The pink-robed guard knelt over his companion who had been felled by Hunt's first rock. Remo moved past him and into the room beyond.

Winthrop Dalton, V. Rodefer Harrow III, and Cletis Larribee looked up.

"Say, fella, what are you doing here?" asked Dalton.

"Which one of you is expendable?" Remo asked.

"He is," said Dalton, pointing to Harrow.

"He is," said Harrow, pointing to Dalton.

"I pick you," said Remo to Harrow, crushing his skull into his jowls.

"Hey, fella," said Dalton, looking at Harrow's collapsing body. "No need to work your hostility out on us."

"Where is he?"

"Who?"

"The swami."

Dalton pointed to a closed-circuit television set on the wall. It showed Maharaji Gupta Mahesh Dor acknowledge the applause, and step forward to a microphone.

"He's out there," said Dalton. "And we have to go now, so if you'll just get out of our way."

"Who are you?" said Remo to Cletis Larribee. "How come you don't say anything?"

"He'll have plenty to say in just a few minutes," said Dalton. "And if you must know, he is the deputy director of the Central Intelligence Agency."

"What's in the suitcase, pal?" Remo asked Larribee.

"Watch the television," said Dalton huffily. "You'll see it all on there in a few minutes. Come, Cletis, time to go."

Dalton took a step toward the door and then took no more steps as his Adam's apple found itself inextricably entwined with his spinal column. He fell to the floor on top of Harrow.

"You're the big thing that they've been talking about, aren't you?" said Remo.

Larribee, too terrified to speak, could only nod.

"But you're not going to say anything tonight, are you?" said Remo.

Larribee shook his head rapidly from side to side. His voice came back. "Don't worry, pal. I'm not going to say anything."

"Look around you," said Remo, gesturing toward the two bodies. "And don't forget. I'll be watching you."

Larribee nodded. "I won't forget. I won't forget."

"And I'll take the briefcase," said Remo.

"Those are state secrets in there," said Larribee.

"You can have them back as soon as you're done."

On the bandstand before national television, Maharaji Dor was finished detailing the support for his simple message of bliss and happiness that he had gained all over the world, and even from one of America's heartland religions, the Baptists.

"But even more encouraging, even more proof that mine is the way, even a greater display of the power of the truth, is the next man I will introduce to you. A man who knows the secrets of government will tell you about that. Will tell you the truth about your government, and then he will speak about divine truth."

He turned and saw Larribee coming up the steps of the bandstand.

"Ladies and gentlemen, listen now to this message from the deputy director of your country's Central Intelligence Agency. My friend and follower, Cletis . . . uh . . . Cletis is how I know him."

He waved his arm toward Larribee in a gesture of greeting. There were a few boos, a few small smatterings of applause. Mostly the audience sat stunned.

Larribee, looking neither left nor right, brushed by Maharaji Dor and took the microphone. He gazed out over the crowd. He saw the thousands of faces. He realized millions more were watching on coast-to-coast live television.

He put down the microphone, then remembered Remo's hard eyes, and raised it to his face again. He opened his mouth and, softly, began to croak:

"What a friend we have in Jesus,
"All our sins and grief to bear."

As he moved along the old gospel song, his voice grew stronger. He closed his eyes to imagine himself back in the choir loft of the Monumental Baptist Church at Willows Landing.

"What a privilege to carry,
"Everything to God in prayer."

173

Maharaji Dor jumped foward and ripped the microphone from Larribee's hand.

"And now you know," he screamed into it. "You can't trust the CIA." He threw the microphone to the wooden floor of the bandstand. The loud crack resounded through the stadium.

"I'm going home," Dor shouted. "I'm going back to Patna." He stamped his foot like an angry child. "You hear me? I'm going back."

"Go back, you bum," came a shout from the audience.

"Yeah, go back, you bum. Who needs you?"

The stadium became a crescendo of booing, as Remo moved up to where Chiun and Joleen stood.

At the same moment, Elton Snowy, who had carefully worked his way through the infield carrying his bogus bag of chicken, came around the platform. He saw his daughter.

"Joleen," he shouted.

She looked up. "Daddy," she yelled with happiness.

Snowy came running toward her, and she threw her arms around him. He tried to hug her back, but the bag of bombed chicken was in the way.

"Here, pal, take this," he said to Remo, thrusting the bag to him.

Remo shrugged, took the bag, then opened Larribee's briefcase and stuck the bag inside. He snapped the briefcase shut again.

"I missed you so much," Snowy said.

"Me, too, Daddy." She stepped back. "Daddy, I want you to meet the man I love."

Snowy looked over her shoulder at Remo. Remo shrugged, a who-me shrug. Joleen turned around and waved her hand toward Chiun. "He is my real master," she said, "And I love him."

"Joleen, honey," said her father. "I love you. You know that."

She nodded.

He brought a right hand up and punched her crisp on the chin. The girl collapsed in his arms. "But you ain't marrying no dink." He lifted the girl in his arms and began to walk toward one of the stadium exits.

"What did that mean?" Chiun asked Remo.

"That's racism, Chiun," Remo answered.

"Racism? I thought racism was something to do with baseball."

"No. He just doesn't want his daughter to marry a Korean."

"But how will you white people ever improve yourselves if you don't marry up to yellow?" asked Chiun.

"Damned if I know," said Remo. He and Chiun turned, walking in the direction that Maharaji Dor had stomped out in. But when they reached the ramp, Remo saw Larribee still standing behind the bandstand, looking lost and frightened.

"I'll catch up to you," said Remo, and he went back to Larribee.

"Good show," said Remo.

Frightened, Larribee could only nod.

"Here's your briefcase. I think you ought to go home," said Remo.

Larribee nodded again, but did not move. He seemed paralyzed, rooted to the spot.

"Oh, hell," said Remo. "Come on." He took Larribee's arm and pulled him toward one of the stadium exits, moving him quickly through the swirls of confused, angry people now anting their way across the stadium playing surface.

After Larribee was safely in a cab on his way to the airport, Remo slid back through the flow of people to the ramp leading to the maharaji's office.

Except for the bodies of Dalton and Harrow, the first office was empty. The door to the inner office was closed,

175

but as Remo approached it, the door was flung open. Chiun stood there.

"Remo," he said. "I am going to Sinanju."

"I told you, as soon as we're done, I'll try to get it arranged again."

He moved into the room as Chiun said, "No. I mean I am going now."

Remo looked at him, then at Maharaji Dor seated behind the desk, then back at Chiun, who said, "I am joining his employ."

Stunned, Remo was silent a second, then said: "Just like that?"

"Just like that," said Chiun. "I will have my daytime dramas beamed in by satellite. He has promised. And I can visit Sinanju frequently. He has promised. Remo, you didn't get a chance to really know the beautiful people of India, or to see the loveliness of the Indian countryside." He looked at Remo expectantly.

Remo looked back, then said coldly: "If you go, you go alone."

"So be it," said Chiun.

Remo turned and walked away.

"Where are you going?" asked Chiun.

"To get drunk."

CHAPTER SEVENTEEN

Remo was no longer really a drinker.

Six bartenders in San Francisco could swear to that.

In the first bar, he had ordered a shot of Seagram's, and when the bartender brought it, he had raised it to his mouth to slug it down, but the smell had wafted into his nostrils and he could not make himself drink the liquor. He had paid the bartender and left, and next door in another tavern, ordered a beer, and when it came, he had raised it to his lips, but its smell gagged him, and again he paid and left, leaving the drink untouched.

Four more times he tried, but the Sinanju disciplines were too strong to be broken that easily, that recklessly, and besides over each glass, he heard's Chiun's lecturing voice:

"Alcohol is for pickling things that are dead. Or people who wish to be."

Or: "Beer is made from a grain that only cows can consume, and even they need two stomachs to manage the task."

So instead, Remo walked the night, angry and sad,

hoping that someone would try to mug him, preferably an army company, so that he would have a way to work off his fury.

But no one did, and Remo walked the entire night before returning to his suite, overlooking a golf course near Golden Gate Park.

He looked around, hoping to see Chiun putter out from the bedroom, but the apartment was empty and echo-still.

Then the phone rang.

Remo had it to his ear before the first ring stopped.

"Good work, Remo," Smith said.

"Oh, it's you."

"Yes. Everything seems to be under control."

"Well, I'm glad. I'm really glad for you," Remo said. "You don't know how glad."

"Except there's one thing. Larribee was blown up this morning in his car, driving to his home in Washington."

"Good for him. At least he found a way out of this mess."

"You had nothing to do with it?" Smith asked suspiciously.

"No. I just wish I had."

"All right. By the way, you'll be interested in knowing. That security leak that I thought we had in Folcroft? Well, it turned out to be just an underpaid little computer clerk. Seems he followed the maharaji, and one day just couldn't restrain himself and pumped a message into the computer. Very amusing, but really nothing . . ."

"Smitty," Remo interrupted.

"What?"

"Go piss up a rope."

Remo slammed down the telephone. He looked around the apartment again, as if Chiun might have sneaked in while he was on the phone, but the silence was total, overpowering, so strong it rang in his ears, and Remo went over

178

to break the silence, and flipped on Chiun's portable color television set.

The transistorized set broke instantly into picture and sound. It was the morning news, and an announcer with a smile said:

"Maharaji Gupta Mahesh Dor held a press conference this morning in the Holiday Inn in San Francisco and announced that he will never again set foot in America.

"This came on the heels of last night's highly publicized Blissathon in Kezar Stadium, which turned into a noisy, violent fiasco in which at least three persons died, victims of mob violence."

The announcer's voice faded and then came film of Dor's press conference, and when Remo saw Dor's fat face with the incipient mustache, he growled, deep in his throat, drew back his right fist, and . . .

Tap, tap, tap.

Remo stopped. There was a tapping on the door. The sound was familiar, as if it were made by long fingernails.

Remo's face brightened, and he brought his right arm to his face to brush away moisture that he had not realized was there.

He opened the door. Chiun stood there.

"Chiun. How are you?"

"How should I be? I have come for my television set. I didn't want to leave that." He brushed by Remo and entered the room. "See, already you are using it, wearing it out while my back is turned."

"Take it and get the fuck out," Remo said.

"I will. I will. But first I had better check it. Not that

179

I think you would steal anything, but, well, one never knows with Americans."

As Remo watched, Chiun stood alongside the set, laboriously counting the knobs, and then counting them again, and then leaning over the vented back of the set and peering inside to examine machinery that Remo knew he did not understand. Occasionally he went "hmmmm."

"I should have killed that fat-faced creep," said Remo.

Chiun snorted and continued his inspection.

"You know why I let him live?" Remo asked. "Because I knew this time you were serious, and he was your new employer. And I wouldn't make a hit on your employer."

Chiun looked up, shaking his head sadly. "You are crazy," he said. "Like all white men. I am sick of whites. That girl was in love with me, and that lunatic with the bag of chicken punched her. And here I thought, it was only baseball that was racist. And Smith. And . . ."

"Screw it. I should have finished that frog. If I ever see him again, I will."

"Typical white thinking. Doing something in such a manner as to cause more harm than good. Do you know that Indians get very upset when Indians die in foreign lands? Particularly rich Indians. And yet you would go ahead, just like that, poof, and kill him. Well, fortunately you will not commit that folly. I have killed him, and in such a way that sloppiness will never be attached to the name of Sinanju."

Chiun folded his arms and stared challengingly at Remo.

"But I just saw him alive. On the television set."

"Nothing ever sinks into the white racist mind. When a hand strikes the right point in the neck, is the person dead?"

"Yes," said Remo.

"No," said Chiun. "It means that the person is going to die. He is not dead yet. It takes time for the brain to be disconnected from the rest of the body. Some blows are fast. Some blows are slower, and death takes longer. Like long enough for him to return home to India, before he dies of bad kidneys."

"I don't believe it," Remo said. "You would have had to make that kind of stroke without his knowing about it."

"And you are a fool. Have you learned nothing? If a man gets a bump, and then nothing happens immediately that day, he assumes it is healed and was nothing to worry about. You can bump into someone openly and inflict that kind of wound. And in two days there will be no pain, and in two months he will be dead. Any fool could learn that. Any fool but you, that is. Remo, you are a disgrace. A pathetic incompetent desecration of the name Sinanju. I saw you last night using a stone on that Frenchman whose family was trained by my family. A disgrace. A fiasco. Rubbish."

"But . . ."

"That settles it. I cannot leave you at this level of stupidity. More work is needed to bring you to even the lowest level of accomplishment. Much more work. And I am afraid I must be here to supervise it. Such is the burden of the dedicated teacher, who dares to try to train fools to come in out of the rain."

"Chiun," Remo said, a smile beginning to crease his face. "I can't say . . . I can't . . ."

But Chiun had changed the channel from the news broadcast of Maharaji Dor to an early morning soap opera, and he raised a hand for silence as he stared at the set.

And Remo was silent, because no one disturbs the Master of Sinanju during his momentary respite of beauty.

"Practice your breathing," Chiun said. "I will get to you later. And then we can discuss our trip to Sinanju. That is, if you and the other racists have not already forgotten your promise."

Remo turned to the door.

"Where are you going?" Chiun asked.

"To rent a submarine," said Remo.

the Executioner

The gutsiest, most exciting hero in years.
Imagine a guy at war with the Godfather
and all his Mafioso relatives! He's rough,
he's deadly, he's a law unto himself —
nothing and nobody stops him!

THE EXECUTIONER SERIES by DON PENDLETON

Order		Title	Book #	Price
———	# 1	WAR AGAINST THE MAFIA	P401	$1.25
———	# 2	DEATH SQUAD	P402	1.25
———	# 3	BATTLE MASK	P403	1.25
———	# 4	MIAMI MASSACRE	P404	1.25
———	# 5	CONTINENTAL CONTRACT	P405	1.25
———	# 6	ASSAULT ON SOHO	P406	1.25
———	# 7	NIGHTMARE IN NEW YORK	P407	1.25
———	# 8	CHICAGO WIPEOUT	P408	1.25
———	# 9	VEGAS VENDETTA	P409	1.25
———	#10	CARIBBEAN KILL	P410	1.25
———	#11	CALIFORNIA HIT	P411	1.25
———	#12	BOSTON BLITZ	P412	1.25
———	#13	WASHINGTON I.O.U.	P413	1.25
———	#14	SAN DIEGO SIEGE	P414	1.25
———	#15	PANIC IN PHILLY	P415	1.25
———	#16	SICILIAN SLAUGHTER	P416	1.25
———	#17	JERSEY GUNS	P417	1.25
———	#18	TEXAS STORM	P418	1.25
———	#19	DETROIT DEATHWATCH	P419	1.25
———	#20	NEW ORLEANS KNOCKOUT	P475	1.25
———	#21	FIREBASE SEATTLE	P499	1.25
———	#22	HAWAIIAN HELLGROUND	P625	1.25

AND MORE TO COME . . .

TO ORDER

Please check the space next to the book/s you want, send this order form
together with your check or money order, include the price of the book/s
and 25¢ for handling and mailing, to:

**PINNACLE BOOKS, INC. / P.O. Box 4347
Grand Central Station/New York, N.Y. 10017**

☐ CHECK HERE IF YOU WANT A FREE CATALOG.

I have enclosed $_____check_____or money order_____as payment
in full. No C.O.D.'s.

Name_____

Address_____

City_____State_____Zip_____
(Please allow time for delivery.)

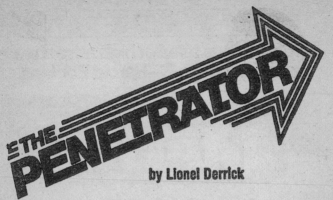

by Lionel Derrick

Mark Hardin. Discharged from the army, after service in Vietnam. His military career was over. But *his* war was just beginning. His reason for living and reason for dying become the same—to stamp out crime and corruption wherever he finds it. He is deadly; he is unpredictable; and he is dedicated. He is The Penetrator!

Read all of him in:

Order		Title	Book No.	Price
_____	#1	THE TARGET IS H	P236	.95
_____	#2	BLOOD ON THE STRIP	P237	.95
_____	#3	CAPITOL HELL	P318	.95
_____	#4	HIJACKING MANHATTAN	P338	.95
_____	#5	MARDI GRAS MASSACRE	P378	.95
_____	#6	TOKYO PURPLE	P434	$1.25
_____	#7	BAJA BANDIDOS	P502	$1.25
_____	#8	THE NORTHWEST CONTRACT	P540	$1.25
_____	#9	DODGE CITY BOMBERS	P627	$1.25